DATE			

The SECRET LIFE of
DILLY McBEAN

The SECRET LIFE of
DILLY McBEAN

by Dorothy Haas

Bradbury Press

NEW YORK

Bradbury Press
An Affiliate of Macmillan, Inc.
866 Third Avenue, New York, NY 10022
Collier Macmillan Canada, Inc.
Manufactured in the United States of America
The text of this book is set in 12 pt. Caledonia
4 6 8 0 9 7 5

Library of Congress Cataloging-in-Publication Data
Haas, Dorothy F. The secret life of Dilly McBean.
Summary: After being orphaned at an early age and spending
years in boarding schools, Dilly begins a new life in a real
house in a small town, developing secret magnetic powers
under the tutelage of a kindly professor, until he is kidnapped by a madman who plans to control the world with
a computer. [1. Orphans—Fiction. 2. Magnetism—Fic-
tion] I. Title. PZ7.H1124Se 1986 [Fic] 86-8255
ISBN 0-02-738200-1

For my godchildren
Sally, Paul, Anne, Elizabeth, Jill, and Clarinda—
and now Peter.

DILLY McBEAN was being raised by a bank. And Dilly McBean was magnetic. The bank didn't know Dilly was magnetic. Only he knew that.

The Commercial Chemical & Corn Trust & Savings Bank sent Dilly—nicely clothed, and with a generous weekly allowance—to school each fall and to camp each summer. One of the assistant teachers from whichever school always delivered him to camp, putting him into the hands of a camp counselor, saying something like, "So long, old chap. Have a great summer. Now, you feel free to go ahead and duck this here camp counselor." The assistant teacher would laugh heartily at his own feeble joke and wink over Dilly's head at the camp counselor. Then Dilly would watch the assistant teacher leave, going away to his own home and family and vacation.

In the fall, after Dilly had spent a damp summer without ducking anybody, he would hang around the main lodge and watch as families came to pick up the other kids. Fathers would clap their sons on the shoulder and make some kind of joke. "Hey, there, Tiger! What've they been feeding you— Vigoro? You've shot up like a tree." And mothers would groan and wail, "None of your school clothes will fit. And whoever gave you that haircut?"

After everybody had cleared out, and the maintenance crew was driving around in the camp jeep, putting tables inside buildings and winterizing the lodge, one of the camp counselors would take Dilly in tow and deliver him to school. His next school.

The Commercial Chemical & Corn Trust & Savings Bank did its best in a businesslike way. When Dilly was small, they sent him to camp to learn to swim and canoe. When he got a little older, he found himself at computer camp . . . music camp . . . martial arts camp. He learned a lot, those summers. But he didn't learn to climb mountains.

Dilly dreamed, sometimes, of mountain climbing. He liked to think of scrambling up the sheer face of a peak nobody else had ever climbed and seeing, from the top, far-off forests and meadows and eagles riding the wind. But of course he understood that mountain climbing was not possible. Not for now. And he did have to stay somewhere, at a school or camp. He could see that. He couldn't exactly live in a safety deposit box at the bank!

Dilly's schools were as varied as the camps. One year he went to a school that built its studies around seamanship. He learned to crew on a schooner and handle different kinds of sails. The following term he went out west to school. All the kids had horses. Dilly had one, too—an Appaloosa.

But to Dilly, horses, sailing, music, whatever, didn't make much difference. A camp was a camp and a school was a school. Nobody had ever thought of sending him to a mountain-climbing school.

Dilly was being raised by a bank because one long-ago autumn day, a truck carrying an enormous load of hay had stopped at a certain traffic light. Dilly's mother and father, the top down on their car, had stopped at the same light. They were on their way to take Dilly's dog, Clyde Alexander, to the vet's for shots. Slowly, the load of hay on the truck had started to lean. Lazily, like a slow-motion movie, the hay had leaned down . . . down . . . down . . . onto the car. Awful!

Nobody told Dilly, of course, how truly awful it had been. He was at the time just a small boy who had been left at home one day to shake off a pesky cold and suddenly was an orphan, with no grand-parents, no uncles, no aunts, no cousins. Everybody was especially kind to him. Cook gave him ice cream whenever he wanted it, even before dinner. Mamie, the upstairs maid, stopped making him pick up his toys. Mrs. Carmichael, the housekeeper, let him stay up at night as late as he liked.

Things went on like that for a while. Then one day the people from the bank came to see Dilly. They looked around and said "tut tut" and "hrumph" and "this will never do." "The boy needs male supervision," they said. "He needs other boys to play with," they said. "He needs an education befitting a child of his means," they said.

And so began Dilly's migrations between schools and camps.

In time his memory of home faded. Even his memory of his mother and father grew dim. He had photographs of them, of course. But the people in the pictures were stiff, somehow not like their real selves.

Dilly remembered his mother's smile. Not her face, exactly, just her smile, hanging there all by itself behind his closed eyelids. The smile made Dilly feel as though he was sitting in sunlight.

And he remembered his father's deep, rumbling voice talking about things that were hard to understand and making them easy. Where the sun went at night. Why grass was green. How electricity flowed through a wire to make a light bulb glow. How magnetic objects drew things to themselves. This last was important to Dilly.

Dilly's magnetism wasn't the sort that makes people say of someone, "He's got a magnetic personality." Not the sort that makes people turn toward a certain person, the most popular person in a crowd. No. Dilly's magnetism was the kind that picks up things. His hands were magnetic. Paper clips, nails, pins, tools just stuck to his fingers if he wasn't careful to keep the magnetism under control.

Dilly remembered one time, when he was little, playing around with his magnetism. He had lifted Clyde Alexander into his red wagon and was walking along the garden path, his hand held out just in front of the metal handle. The wagon had rolled along smoothly after him.

His father had come bounding out of the laboratory. "Son," he said, "that's a lot of fun, I know."

Dilly beamed up at him. "Hi, Papa. I'm giving Clyde Alexander a ride. He likes that."

Indeed, Clyde Alexander seemed to. He was grinning a doggy grin, his tail drumming happily on the wagon.

Dr. McBean folded his long length down to Dilly size. "This is a game you and Mother and I know about," he said seriously. "But it's our secret."

Dilly listened soberly. He nodded his head.

"You're beginning to grow up," said Dr. McBean. "I'll be teaching you more about this game. But for now I'm asking for your word of honor that you won't play the game in front of anyone but Mother and me. Not in front of the household help. Not in front of the yardmen. Not anywhere at all where somebody else might see you."

Dilly had promised. He had kept his word. Unhappily, the accident with the hay had happened soon afterward, so he never learned all those things his father had promised to teach him. But to this day, he had kept his word. He had never talked to anyone about his magnetism.

Of course, odd things did occasionally happen.

Like the time in craft class at Camp Potawatomi, when he was really thinking hard about a belt he was making. He and Pinky Jameson both reached for a leather punch at the same time. The punch flicked up into Dilly's hand.

Pinky looked startled. But their hands had been so close together, he didn't seem sure of what he had just seen. He shrugged. "Well, I get it next," he said.

It had been a close call and reminded Dilly that he had to be careful, that he had to keep a part of his mind tuned in on the power in his hands.

And then there was the time he dropped the box of nails. That was the year he spent at Roughing It ('Where boys become men").

Without thinking, he had knelt, reached out, and started to let the nails pop up against his fingers. A noise made him look up. One of the teachers was coming around the end of the workbench. Carefully, Dilly had lowered his hand to the floor and scooped the nails into a pile. Then he'd crawled around picking up the stray ones with his fingers, instead of doing it the easy way by letting them flip up against his hand.

He hadn't gone back to Potawatomi. Nor to Roughing It. Nor to any of the other camps or schools where the little accidents happened.

Time passed, though, and as Dilly gained somewhat firmer control of the magnetism which was his gift, the accidents became fewer.

This particular summer was much like the others. Dilly had been dropped off at Camp Wabanaki by the assistant headmaster of the Brandywine Whole Boy Developmental Academy. In addition to the usual swimming and riding, he had spent a lot of time in woodcraft class. He had made two boxes with lids that fit snugly. And he was trying to carve an eagle in flight, the kind he imagined soared above the mountains he wished he could climb.

But while Dilly was swimming and canoeing and carving, something was going on that would change his whole future. It began with a meeting.

THE OFFICERS of the trust department of the Commercial Chemical & Corn Trust & Savings Bank were meeting to talk about Dilly. As a rule, the officers met by themselves. But today someone had joined them.

The man, Homer Orbed, was short and round. A fringe of ginger-colored hair surrounded the dome of his very shiny head. His weathered face was round. His nose, a button, was round. Round gold-rimmed glasses enlarged his round sea-blue eyes.

He looked about at the officers seated at the polished mahogany table. "As you know," he said, "I have spent a number of years out of the country."

"Research, wasn't it?" asked the Executive Vice-President. He puffed at his pipe as he spoke. The pipe made little *bupping* noises. "In"—*bup bup*—"Antarctica? On penguins"—*bup bup*—"didn't you say?" *Bup.*

Mr. Orbed nodded. "The project was a long one. Didn't give me much time stateside. But now I am back and able to pick up on things that have been on my mind."

The First Vice-President fingered her floppy, silk bow tie. "Judge Tenley called last week. He explained your interest in the McBean boy and said future decisions about his education will rest with you."

The Executive Vice-President was quick to add, "Naturally we will continue to handle the boy's finances."

The Assistant Vice-President leaned forward. An earnest frown creased his brow. "I trust you have had no concern about the quality of the boy's education?"

Mr. Orbed made a steeple of his fingertips. "Excellent schools. Fine. Fine." He settled more comfortably into his leather armchair. "You have seen to it that the boy had the supervised environment needed by a very young child. But now I have something rather different in mind. Tell me. What became of the family's possessions?"

With the eraser end of her pointed yellow pencil the First Vice-President flicked through the papers that lay, four-square neat, in front of her. "The house itself was sold, of course." The yellow pencil stopped near the bottom of the stack of papers. "Ah. Here it is. Everything is with Acme Storage."

The Assistant Vice-President looked puzzled. "But what do the household furnishings have to do with school?"

Mr. Orbed tapped his gold pen thoughtfully on the mirrorlike surface of the table. "I have decided," he said, looking from one to another of the interested faces, "to enroll the boy in public school."

Three mouths fell open.

"Public school!"

"Appropriate, do you feel, for a boy of his means?"

Bup.

"Shouldn't he attend school with youngsters of his financial standing?"

Looking pleased with the effect of his statement, Mr. Orbed closed his leather portfolio. He placed the gold pen tidily on top. "My intention is"—he held up a pudgy finger—"one, to scout out a nice, smallish town with good schools and a countryside where a boy can ramble. Two"—up went another plump finger—"I intend to set up a residence there, furnished with things from the boy's home. And" —a third chubby finger lifted—"I intend to locate a reliable couple to look after him."

Three stunned faces stared at him. The room was still.

"It's time," Mr. Orbed said firmly. "The lad will benefit from a greater measure of freedom. And where can he best try his wings than in a nice, small town!"

And so it was that, on a glowing day in late summer, a mildly dazed Dilly McBean found himself on a plane winging eastward. He was on his way to Hennessy Depot.

*Dusk was settling over a brush-tangled slope
in a mountainous region of the country . . .*

*as a figure in a gray coat, the collar turned up,
made its way along a barely visible path among
the trees. The man paused from time to time to
glance over his shoulder. Assuring himself that he
was unobserved, he tugged his hat lower over his
eyes and continued on his way.*

*Arriving at last at a thicket of laurel, he paused
again, looking around. Then he thrust aside the
greenery. Behind it, in an embankment of earth
and rock that seemed to be a part of the moun-
tainside, was a door. He stepped toward it and
placed a card in a hidden slot. Words were murmured from within. Softly, the man uttered a
password. The door slid open and he entered.
Soundlessly, the door closed behind him.*

He stood in a large room, a hall. A fountain played in a pool at the center of the room, the jets lifting and falling in shifting patterns. Comfortable chairs and couches stood around the room in groups. A large empty picture frame dominated one wall. Beneath it was a computer terminal.

The room was dimly lit. In contrast, the room beyond, visible through a window in the far wall, was brightly lighted. Several lab-coated workers moved among computer equipment in the room.

Except for the muted swoosh of the fountain, the scene was eerily still. Then a voice spoke. "Ah, Master Operative Gorey." A figure stepped out of the shadows.

The man was not overly large. Pipe-stem legs and skinny arms protruded from his sleeveless black jacket like the limbs of a jointed puppet. His hair, a wild wiry mass, looked as though it had been electrified. His eyes—amber, shrewd— bulged. He advanced on silent feet. "You bring me fodder for the Great Harmonizer?"

The master operative placed his briefcase on a table. "Dr. Keenwit. Greetings. Yes. I bring information."

Dr. Keenwit stood over the briefcase rubbing his hands, waiting for it to be opened. The bulging eyes glittered.

BEFORE THE PLANE LANDED, the flight attendant asked Dilly and Camp Counselor Abe Ford
to remain in their seats until the other passengers
had deplaned. They were, she said, being met.

Dilly watched as people passed through first class
and exited out the forward door, his eyes riveted
on the opening. Mr. Orbed, he was fairly sure, would
be entering there.

Weeks before, Mr. Orbed had come to Camp
Wabanaki to talk to Dilly about his plans. Dilly was
shocked at being consulted. That had never happened before. But as they talked, he thought he
might like giving public school a try.

He was equaliy startled to find himself sitting with
someone who seemed to take a personal interest in
him. He studied the round little man, who said he
had been a professional friend of Dilly's father.

"You don't remember me, do you," said Mr. Orbed.
Dilly shook his head.

"Not surprising," said Mr. Orbed. "You didn't see me that often." He set aside the gold-headed walking stick he carried, reached into his vest pocket, and withdrew a gold watch. "This might trigger a memory." He held it out.

Dilly took the watch, running a finger over the chased design of a quail. A shadow of remembrance stirred.

"Snap it open," said Mr. Orbed.

Dilly released the catch. The lid lifted to reveal the face of the watch.

"It has an alarm," said Mr. Orbed, reaching out to show him. "Press that."

Dilly touched the button. A bell chimed softly.

Suddenly he was back in a living room filled with grown-ups in evening dress. Wearing his night clothes, he had been brought in to say good night. One of those grown-ups had let Dilly look at his watch and make the little chime ring.

"I do remember!" said Dilly. He grinned at the man. "I mean, I remember your watch."

Mr. Orbed had laughed. "You were very small at the time."

After Mr. Orbed left, Dilly had a great deal to think about. He wondered what it would be like to go to school every morning and go home each afternoon. He wondered what it would be like to live in a house, not in a school dormitory. And he wondered if Mr. Orbed knew about his magnetism. Could that be? But Mr. Orbed had not mentioned it. Nor had Dilly, who still remembered the promise made to his father so long ago.

And so it wasn't exactly a stranger who now stepped through the door and came to Dilly, holding out his hand. They shook, man to man.

"I have a car waiting," said Mr. Orbed. "We still have a distance to travel." He turned to Abe Ford. "My thanks for accompanying Dilloway. I'll take over from here."

"The luggage," said the camp counselor. "I'll—"

Mr. Orbed held up a hand. "No need. Just let me have the baggage checks. The bank has assigned me a gofer. He can handle all that."

"Well, then, if you say so," said the camp counselor, handing him the checks. He turned and clapped a hand on Dilly's shoulder. "It's been great knowing you, pal. Remember. Be a credit to—"

"Camp Wabanaki," said Dilly. "You bet."

Dilly followed Mr. Orbed off the plane. The last he saw of Abe, the camp counselor was trading jokes with the flight attendant.

In short order, Dilly and Mr. Orbed were seated in the comfortable backseat of a limousine. Jepson Whirtby, the young and eager-to-please trainee from the Commercial Chemical & Corn Trust & Savings Bank, sat in front, next to the driver. He spoke over his shoulder to Dilly as the car moved away from the terminal building. "If I can be of help in any way, just let me know. I think, I trust"—he glanced hopefully at Mr. Orbed—"I have proven helpful to Mr. Orbed."

Mr. Orbed smiled quietly in response.

They left the airport behind and soon were gliding smoothly along twisting, turning roads among tree-shadowed hills. At every curve there was a surprise. The white rush of a waterfall. A bed of ferns. A flash of open space that revealed more and higher hills beyond. These were old hills, rubbed low by time and weather. And the road was old, too, etched over and around the hills by people and cars and, long ago, horses and oxen and wagons.

Shafts of sunlight in among the trees invited Dilly's eyes into the woodland depths. He liked what he saw. He was going to enjoy exploring these hills. At the moment, though, his attention was divided. A question had filled his mind since Mr. Orbed's visit to Camp Wabanaki.

"What were my mother and father like?" he asked.

"You have pictures of them, of course," said Mr. Orbed.

"Oh, sure," said Dilly. "But I mean, what were they really like?"

Mr. Orbed answered slowly, reaching back into his memory.

"Handsome. You rather favor your mother, I think, though I suspect you're going to be very tall, like your father. Your mother read a lot, always had a book tucked under her arm. She loved flowers. Raised them. Did interesting things with roses, grafting them for new varieties. She played the flute. Your father played the violin. Sometimes when I was there they played together, after dinner."

Dilly remembered, suddenly, lying in bed at night listening to music coming from downstairs. He hadn't thought of it until that very moment.

"Your father was unusually tall," Mr. Orbed continued. "An excellent skier. Had a quick mind. He could add five-digit figures in his head faster than I could do them on a calculator."

Dilly had a growing sense of acquaintanceship with these people he remembered so faintly, a good feeling of connectedness to someone.

They were quiet for a time as they looked out at the changing scenery. They were moving higher into the hills now. A scarlet bird flashed through the dappled shadows. A stream appeared out of nowhere, bubbled over a rocky bed beside the road, then disappeared as suddenly as it had appeared.

"This is roaming country," observed Mr. Orbed. "Like to roam, do you?"

Jepson Whirtby seemed to have an ear trained on what was being said in the back of the car. His head swiveled. "I looked for that quality in searching out this place," he said. "A place where a boy can roam—that's what you said you wanted me to find, sir. Hennessy Depot is made to order."

"Yes-yes." Dilly was to learn that "yes-yes" was Mr. Orbed's all-purpose response to remarks that didn't require much of an answer. Mr. Orbed put the question again. "Like to wander about? Tramp through the woods? Find birds' nests? That sort of thing?"

"Well, after the birds move out," answered Dilly. Mr. Orbed smiled.

"I do like to hike," Dilly admitted. And he told Mr. Orbed about some of the more interesting hikes he had taken at Camp Wabanaki. "It was always sort of crowded, though," he added. "The counselors wanted us to go out in groups." Dilly had liked to slip away by himself when he could, walking with sure, quiet feet, seeing far more of the life of the woods than was possible with a bunch of noisy boys.

"You'll have plenty of open space for hiking around Hennessy Depot," said Mr. Orbed. "Forest lands surround it. The town was once the center of a major lumbering operation."

"Named after a lumber baron," said Jepson Whirtby. "As a matter of fact, your new home was once owned by Hennessy himself."

Your home. Dilly tried out the word in his mind. Home. It was meaningless, just a word. His forehead puckered as he tried to remember the only home he ever had.

His memories were like pieces of a puzzle. He could recall sitting at a table and eating, but he couldn't remember the table itself, or what the dining room looked like. He could recall lying in bed —there was something about a lamp—but he couldn't remember the bedroom.

He had other such bits of memory, too. But the pieces of the puzzle didn't fit together. They didn't make a whole picture of his long-ago home.

Dilly was quiet during the rest of the drive. He felt Mr. Orbed's eyes on him from time to time. The look was penetrating, kindly, yet reserved. Occasionally Mr. Orbed said something about the passing scenery that Dilly could answer or not, as he chose.

Jepson Whirtby, on the other hand, kept up a running commentary. He talked about Hennessy Depot as though he himself could take credit for its charm. "Actually, I know it rather well," he said with self-satisfaction. "I've heard a great deal about it from, uh—" He didn't finish the sentence. "The house is utterly charming."

His talk was sprinkled with self-importance and

"sirs." Dilly quickly sensed that it was intended to impress rather than inform. And that it was meant for Mr. Orbed's ears. Jepson Whirtby thirsted for the older man's approval.

As they entered town, Dilly leaned forward, taking in the place. It did look old. The streets were wide. The trunks of the trees lining them were heavy, thick with moss on their north curves, and grew into massive crowns high overhead. There were a lot of wrought-iron fences. The houses, all big and looking as though they had been there a long time, sat well back from the sidewalks.

The car turned at a brick-paved drive, passed under trees that shaded a lawn, and slowed to a stop before a rambling frame house. The house, the color of goldenrod, was made up of porches and sunporches, carved pillars and cornices, bay windows, towers, gables and cupolas. Anything that could contribute to the glory of a house by the standards of another day had been added to this one.

Jepson Whirtby sprang from the car and opened the back door. Mr. Orbed stepped out and Dilly followed him, looking at this amazing house.

"Your new home." Jepson Whirtby beamed. His manner said that he expected Dilly to jump up and down and yell "fan-*tas*-tic!"

But Dilly had learned long ago to reserve judgment until he could make up his own mind about wherever he happened to be set down. "Wow!" he said softly. "Some house!" Whatever that meant.

A look of understanding crossed Mr. Orbed's face. His lips quirked upward.

But Jepson Whirtby took the words as a compliment. "I knew you'd like it."

The front door opened. The man who stood there wore the gray jacket of a houseman. His shock of inky hair was the blackest Dilly had ever seen, and his eyes disappeared under bushy, black brows. "Afternoon, folks," he said in measured tones. He looked beyond Whirtby and bowed slightly to Mr. Orbed.

"Good to see you again, Blackpool," said Mr. Orbed. He nodded to the woman who hovered behind him. "And you, Mrs. Blackpool." He draped an arm over Dilly's shoulders and drew him into the hall.

"The Blackpools will be taking care of things," he explained. "If there's anything you want, just let them know."

The Blackpools looked agreeable, and Dilly looked agreeable, and everybody smiled at everyone else.

Then they went on a tour of the house. Blackpool led the way, opening doors and turning on lights. Mrs. Blackpool fluttered after him, straightening shades and flicking at invisible specks of dust with a corner of her apron.

Dilly liked what he saw. He felt comfortable. The

house was new to him, of course, but he had a sense of being in welcoming surroundings. That flowered chair—was that the one he used to curl up in with his mother while she read to him? And that seascape above the fireplace—did he once like to pretend he could sail out of the picture to some faraway place on that full-rigged schooner?

In the library, he pulled a book from the shelves. It was on astronomy. He flicked it open. Written on the flyleaf was a name. Octavious D. McBean. Dilly ran a finger over the name. His father had touched this very page!

In the butler's pantry, Mrs. Blackpool lifted the lid from a yellow jar on the counter. "Cookies," she said shyly. "Boys should have cookies. I made these this morning."

Dilly bit into one. It was without a doubt the best chocolate chip cookie he had ever tasted.

He followed the adults up the broad, curving stairs to the second floor, hugging the book, munching on another cookie. Upstairs were bedrooms and dressing rooms and a den with an oversized TV screen. Almost everything in the rooms, except the TV, had a dreamlike familiarity.

Then Blackpool opened a door and Dilly stepped into another room. He stopped, his feet glued to the floor.

In one corner was a youth bed, neatly covered by a quilt made of colored squares. Each square contained a patchwork picture of something he had once liked—a black-and-white dog, a train, a flag, a red wagon.

Dazed, he stood rooted in the doorway. That toy chest! That rocking chair! Under the windows was a blue sleeping bag made to look like a gym shoe. He remembered sliding into that sleeping bag.

The bookshelves were filled with his little-kid books. On top of the shelves was a train.

"Hey, will you look at that!" He bounded across the room, forgetting himself and his magnetism, reaching for the engine. It leaped up from the track and stuck to his fingers.

For a sickening moment he thought the adults had seen. Then he realized they were directly behind him, still in the doorway. His body blocked their view.

"I wonder if it still works," he said with elaborate carelessness, setting it back on the tracks, withdrawing the power into his fingertips. The engine stayed put.

On the bedside table was a lamp. And now he remembered what it was he had liked about that lamp. "Look at this," he said, to further distract the grown-ups.

He touched the switch. The base of the lamp, a dark blue globe, lit up from within. Pinprick stars glittered. The planets tracked each other on their appointed paths. A shooting star burst into life, flashed around the globe, and faded.

"Boy, did I like this when I was little," said Dilly. "I used to watch it at night until I fell asleep."

He turned off the lamp and looked around. Yes, he remembered everything here. But he couldn't sleep in this little-kid room!

Mr. Orbed seemed to read his mind. "A little young for you now, is it?" he asked.

Dilly nodded. "I guess I'll bunk in one of the other rooms."

"Wherever you're comfortable, lad," said Mr. Orbed. "This is your home."

Dilly closed the door behind them, and they finished inspecting the house.

Back in the first-floor hall, Mr. Orbed looked at him closely. "Do you think you can enjoy yourself here?"

Dilly's customary reserve masked his feelings. Would he be happy? How could he know. "It's a very nice house, sir."

"The boy seems pleased, sir," said Jepson Whirtby, as though Dilly wasn't standing right there in front of him.

"Yes-yes." Mr. Orbed ignored the interruption. "I'll ask that question of you in a few months," he said to Dilly. "But in the meantime, settle in. Make friends. Ramble. You've already been enrolled at school. Just present yourself there on opening day. If there's anything you need, let Blackpool here know about it." He made a movement toward the door. "I'll stop in from time to time to see how you're getting on. I'm only an hour's drive away. In the meantime, Whirtby here—"

"J.B.," murmured his assistant. "Feel free to call me J.B."

"—will keep in touch with Blackpool about day-to-day operations."

Then Mr. Orbed went out to the waiting limousine, Jepson Whirtby leaping before him to open the door.

Dilly watched the long black car drive away. When he turned to go inside, he realized he was still hugging his father's book.

Blackpool closed the door. "Dinner's set for six tonight. After today we can serve it any time you want."

Dilly felt himself on the receiving end of a piercing look from under the heavy brows. "Six is okay," he said. "Thanks."

The Blackpools disappeared into the back of the

house. Leaning against the stair railing, stroking the cover of the book, Dilly watched them go. What kind of people were they? It was too soon to tell. People were often nice to you in front of other grown-ups. The proof of things was how they treated you when you were alone with them.

DILLY OPENED HIS EYES the next morning, squirming out of the shaft of sunlight that splashed his face. Yawning, stretching, he looked around the pleasant high-ceilinged room. His glance came to rest on the sky lamp on the bedside table. Paled by the bright light of morning, the stars still twinkled, the comets flashed, the planets moved sedately on their course. It was one of the few things he had carried from his childhood room last night, and he had gone to sleep watching it. A slow smile spread across his face. He reached out and switched it off.

His hand dropped to a battered red dish on the table. He picked it up, fingering the rough toothmarks that edged it. Clyde Alexander's dish. Good old Clyde Alexander.

He set the dish back on the table and rolled out of bed. He slid into his jeans and tugged his favorite striped T-shirt over his head. There were some things he meant to do today. Buy a bicycle. Explore Hennessy Depot. And something else, something special.

He ate breakfast at a small table in the bay window of the dining room, rather than at the formal dining table that stretched the length of the room like a polished highway.

Mrs. Blackpool moved in springy, quick little steps between the pantry and the table, taking away Dilly's empty orange juice glass, filling his milk glass, setting down a plate of scrambled eggs and bacon.

"Be careful, now. This plate is real hot."

Dilly leaned back, away from the plate. "Yes, ma'am."

She turned to leave. "You want anything else, just ring. The bell's next to the flowers, there."

Dilly picked it up, forgetting his food. The bell was brass and had a little carving of a llama on the top. He remembered it! He remembered wondering what it would be like to ride on a llama. He shook it and the bell gave out a pure, high *tinggg*.

"Lunch will be at noon sharp," Mrs. Blackpool added over her shoulder, from the pantry door.

Dilly looked up from the llama. "Yes, ma'am. Only I won't be home for lunch today." Funny, to say *home*.

She raised an eyebrow.

"I'm gonna get a bike," he explained. "Then I'm gonna ride around town and see the school and stuff."

She looked as though she wasn't at all sure that's what he should do. "Well, I suppose that'll be all right," she murmured, biting her lip. "But you tell Blackpool. Do you think you'll want a picnic lunch?"

Dilly shook his head. "I'll stop somewhere and get a hamburger."

The swinging door swished behind her.

Dilly slathered butter on his toast and tackled his bacon and eggs. Good. But eating alone wasn't going to be such a great part of this new setup. It was a little like eating in the school dining hall when everyone else had gone home for the holidays. Dull. But dull.

Mrs. Blackpool bounced back into the dining room as he was finishing, to see if he wanted anything else. Dilly crumpled his napkin and put it on the table. She gathered up the dishes, fixing him with serious eyes. "Don't be late for dinner, now."

Blackpool was waiting out in the drive, leaning against the car. He looked closely at Dilly. "The wife says you're going to buy a bicycle and that you're going to stay away all day. I'm not sure that's such a good idea."

"I do," said Dilly. "If I'm gonna live here, I have to know where places are. Anyway," he added logically, "when I go to school I'll be away all day."

"Different," said Blackpool. "You'll be under supervision. We're supposed to look after you," he explained. "If you just take off for a whole day at a time, looking after you gets to be hard."

Dilly studied the man. There had to be a way to work this out to both his and Blackpool's satisfaction. "Tell you what," he said finally. "If it'll make you feel better, why don't you call Mr. Orbed. You'll see, he'll say it's okay for me to go out rambling. That's what he called it, rambling."

"Well . . ." Blackpool pulled at his chin. "Well . . ."

"I'll phone you at noon," Dilly added. "Let you know where I am."

They left things at that.

As they drove toward the center of town, Blackpool told him the telephone number and Dilly wrote it down. Blackpool had only one more thing to say. "Don't see why you need a bike when you've got a perfectly good car here. I'm glad to drive you wherever you want to go."

Dilly looked at him in surprise. "I can't go to school in a car!" he exclaimed. "The kids would think I was really weird." And besides, there was all that countryside outside of Hennessy Depot waiting to be explored.

THE BIG WHEEL BIKE SHOP was on a narrow street, one in a row of skinny old stores lined up like pickets in a fence. Inside, bikes were stored upright in racks, resting on their back wheels.

On the floor in the center of the shop, a bike was upended on its handlebars and back fender, wheels in the air. The store owner dribbled oil into the sprocket wheel and gave the front wheel a spin before getting up and coming to them. Behind him, the wheel spun, clicking. "Something for you folks?"

Blackpool turned to Dilly, and Dilly ticked off on his fingers. "Ten speed. Racing clips on the pedals. Carrier on the back."

The man pulled bicycles of different kinds from the racks. "You'll need a bell and a light," he said. "Flashers on the wheels are a good idea, too."

Dilly chose a sleek black number and rolled it out of the shop, leaving Blackpool behind to take care of the money part of things. Dilly was more free than he'd ever been in his whole life. Free to move around without a camp counselor or an assistant headmaster tagging after him.

"Now, you know how to get back to the house?" asked Blackpool, coming out of the Big Wheel.

Dilly nodded, nudging a foot into the clip on the left pedal. "I watched where we turned." He pushed off and glided away. "Like I said, I'll phone at noon," he called, looking back over his shoulder.

Blackpool was leaning against the car, stroking his chin, watching . . . watching.

Hennessy Depot was laid out like a wheel, with the town square at the hub. Dilly rode toward the square, entering it from Gertrude Street, and circled it. The square was a pleasant place. At the center was an ornate old bandstand, with flower beds and benches around it.

Old houses edged the square. They had long ago lost their families. Neat signs hung at the doors or swung at the gates. D. GARVEY, REALTOR. P. WIGGINS, M.D. J. PICK, NOTARY PUBLIC.

Dilly circled the square several times, noting that all the streets that fed into it had women's names —Mary, Elizabeth, Josephine, Alice, Margaret, Gertrude. He followed each of the streets until he reached the edge of town, returning to the square each time. On Josephine he found the town park, with its tennis courts and baseball diamond. A game was going on, but he didn't stay to watch. Today was the day he was going to get to know Hennessy Depot.

He found the swimming pool and the ice-skating rink and a hill with a ski lift.

He found the town library, the Amy Frances Hennessy Library. It was in a tall brick Victorian house with a lawn and trees around it, not far from the square.

He found a hobby shop. He found plenty of snack shops. And at last he found the Ida Bertha Hennessy Community School. He rode clear around it, wondering where in the sprawling building his homeroom would be located.

Again he headed back to the square. This time he found a public telephone booth and looked up something in the phone book. Yes. The kind of place he was looking for was in Elm Court. He swung onto his bike and headed toward the nearest snack shop for a cooling Coke and directions.

Elm Court wasn't far from the square, between Margaret and Alice Streets. Dilly slowed in front of Noah Jones's Ark. He propped his bike on its stand, went to the window, and peered inside. A pen with some kittens filled the space. They were frolicking around their sleeping mother.

He opened the door. A bell jangled somewhere in the depths of the shop. Instantly the air was filled with yips, squawks, meows, caws, whistles, and chirps.

He moved past cages of bright-colored birds and bubbling tanks of smoothly gliding tropical fish. The owner was at the back of the shop, moving gently in a rocking chair, yawning and rubbing his eyes.

"Well, m'boy, now that you've woke us all from our after-lunch nap, what can I do for you?"

After lunch!

"Oh, my gosh!" gasped Dilly. "I was supposed to call home. I want to talk to you, but first I've gotta find a telephone."

The man swept a hand toward a desk buried under samples of birdseed and dog food. "Phone's there somewhere. Welcome to use it."

Dilly dug around in his pocket, found the slip of paper with his telephone number, and dialed.

Blackpool answered. "You agreed to call at noon," he said reprovingly. "It's one o'clock. Where are you? What part of town?"

Dilly told him. "In Elm Court. I just remembered. And I'm okay, like I said I'd be."

Blackpool grumbled something about looking after him and finished up with, "Don't be late for dinner."

"Right," Dilly agreed. "I'll be home in plenty of time for dinner."

He wasn't exactly getting off on the best foot with the Blackpools. Apparently meals on time were big stuff with them.

He turned back to Noah Jones.

"I'm looking"—Dilly's brow furrowed as he tried to remember—"for a black-and-white dog, sort of this big." He held his hand waist-high. Then he lowered it, confused. Clyde Alexander had been waist-high when he, Dilly, was five. But how high, exactly, would that be?

Noah Jones was watching him intently. "Sounds like you lost a dog. Did you try putting an ad in the paper?"

Dilly shook his head. "A dog I had a long time ago. I guess I won't find one exactly like him."

"Nope. Dogs are like people, no two alike." Noah Jones heaved himself out of his rocking chair. "Let's see what we've got."

The dogs, most of them puppies, just past babyhood, were in pens out in back of the Ark.

"This poodle here"—Noah Jones picked up a leggy, brown dog—"a good animal."

"Nope, not a poodle." Dilly shook his head. "They're too fancy."

"This here's a standard," said Noah Jones. "Grow up to be a big dog."

But Dilly had moved on. He smoothed the head of a red setter, scratched under the chin of a gray terrier. The dogs wiggled under his hand, tails wagging.

"Ah-oooo," came a mournful sound from behind him. "Ah-oooo." A foghorn would have been rightfully proud of that voice! Dilly swung around.

A short-legged, brown-and-white dog, low-slung in the middle, looked at him with sad, drooping eyes. "Ah-oooo," he moaned.

Dilly laughed. "Some dog!" He went to scratch the long flaps of ears.

Noah Jones strolled after him. "In all conscience, I can't let you have that one, boy. He was the runt of his litter. Never will take any show prizes. And he's downright contrary. Tell him to fetch, he picks up the stick and runs away. Tell him to lie down, he sits up."

"Ah-oooo," belled this improper dog, looking up at Dilly, tail wagging.

Something in the melancholy eyes, something Dilly couldn't name, spoke to him. He scratched behind the silky ears, then held them out like a pair of sails on either side of the sorrowful face. "Hiya, boy. Hiya, Contrary."

He looked up at Noah Jones. "He won't have to win any prizes. And I like him. Will you sell him to me? If I haven't got enough money with me, I'll come back with however much—"

"Money doesn't mean that much to me, boy." Noah Jones folded his hands across his rounded stomach. "I figure I've got to be fair and square with you. This is one peculiar dog. I doubt you can train him to do anything."

"Well, okay, so you've warned me," said Dilly.

"We'll have an understanding, then." Noah Jones lifted the dog out of his pen and led the way back indoors. He set the dog down and found pencil and paper on the cluttered desk. "Here. Write down

your name and address. I'll give you return privi-
leges, because this one's on my conscience. If your
folks say you can't have him, you can bring him back.
Full refund."

Dilly wrote down his name and address.

Noah Jones's left eyebrow lifted when he saw what
Dilly had written. "The old Hennessy place! Well!
Can't say I'm placing this animal in a bad home."

Outside, Dilly knelt and spoke directly to his new
dog, looking into his eyes. "Okay, Contrary. You
are not to follow me when I leave this place. Got
it? You're to turn around"—he pointed to Noah
Jones, standing in the doorway of the Ark—"and go
back into the Ark. Got that? That's an order."

A deep rumble was Contrary's answer.

Dilly swung onto his bike and rolled toward home.
At the corner he stopped and looked down. The
brown-and-white dog was there at his heels. "You
still here?" said Dilly. "I thought I told you to go
back"—he pointed—"to the Ark."

Contrary's tail waved. He looked up at Dilly soulfully. "Ah-oooo."

Every time Dilly glanced over his shoulder, call-
ing, "I said back to the Ark, you," Contrary answered with his Foghorn Special. He followed at
Dilly's heels, rounding corner after corner, his long
ears flapping, his stubby legs a blur. He followed

him through town and angled into the drive after him.

Dilly pulled up at the kitchen door. "What?" he said sternly. "Are you still here?"

Contrary wriggled in reply.

Dilly kicked out the stand on his bike and went to the door. He opened it, pointing back down the drive. "Contrary," he said, "you are absolutely forbidden to come into my house."

Contrary marched past him into the kitchen.

Mrs. Blackpool was stirring something at the table. "My stars," she said, "where did you get that!"

"Mrs. Blackpool," Dilly said formally, "may I present my dog, I think, to you. His name's Contrary McBean. He does exactly the opposite of whatever you tell him."

Mrs. Blackpool flopped into a chair. "Nobody ever said anything about dogs," she wailed.

Contrary went to her and licked her hand.

"Go away, dog," said Mrs. Blackpool. "What's your name? Contrary? Go away. I don't think I like dogs."

Contrary lay down and rested his chin on her shoe.

"He'll need a water dish," said Dilly. "And he's gonna eat with me, next to my chair."

"Ah-oooo," said Contrary.

***That night
in a fog-bound city on the coast . . .***

*figures crept stealthily through a park, one by
one. The collars of their gray coats turned up, the
brims of their gray hats turned down, they descended an embankment and gathered silently under an aged bridge of ornamental design. They
blended, gray shadows, into the gray mist that
shrouded the bridge, the park, the city.*

*Three arrived, and then a fourth dressed in a
natty, double-breasted dark coat. They did not
greet each other. None spoke. They shifted rest-
lessly, waiting.*

*A voice spoke suddenly from the shadows. "Re-
port in. Code names only, if you please."*

*"Blunt here." "O'Mallet here." "Von Pfist here."
The voices were low.*

"Unc-uh," stuttered a fourth voice. "Whir—uh, sorry, Unc-uh—McHammer here." The speaker in the dark coat peered into the shadows. But the fog did not give up its secrets.

"Operative McHammer," said the cool voice. "Your presence here tonight is unusual for someone at your level. However, you sent a message through Contacts that you had information you felt you had to pass along in person."

"Oh, my, yes." McHammer spoke eagerly. "I have obtained a position as trainee with the Commercial Chemical & Corn Trust & Savings Bank. Recently I was able to effect something that will surely be useful.

"The bank handles the affairs of an orphaned child who has been kept in boarding school. Recently, a new guardian was appointed for the boy. I was assigned to assist him. The guardian decided to place the boy in a home of his own in a pleasant small town. In my position as assistant, I was directed to find a town of that description. Naturally, I selected"—he paused for full effect—"Hennessy Depot."

"Most interesting," came the response from the shadows.

"You might consider the boy a secure loan," McHammer continued in a rush. "Your, er, our work must be costly. Were the boy to be picked up and held—"

"Ah, yes, I begin to see."

"—a large sum of money would certainly be paid for his release," McHammer finished triumphantly.

"Original thinking," murmured the cool voice. "In light of this information, Operatives von Pfist, O'Mallet, Blunt, your current assignments are placed on hold. Proceed at once to 'the pleasant small town.' Infiltrate the environment. Maintain a low profile. One week from today, call Contacts for the time and place of our next meeting. I will want facts, facts, facts to assess whether this child can be of use to us."

"But, sir! I will be often on the scene!" Hurt edged McHammer's words. "I can provide you with all the information you need. It was my idea!"

"Amateur!" Was that word whispered? Did it hang in the air?

"Yes?" asked the voice out of the mist. The word was not repeated. He continued. "Congratulations, McHammer, on this unusual plan and your execution of it to this point."

"Thank you, sir." McHammer coughed modestly.

"But you are new to the work. You cannot be expected to recognize all the small signs that go into a successful operation. Continue to be observant. Report everything, no matter how small, through Contacts. And now, please, your reports."

One by one the operatives stepped forward and placed sheaves of paper on the briefcase that lay upon the ground.

"These will be processed," said the voice from the shadows. "If there are questions, Contacts will notify you. We will now disperse, observing the customary precautions."

The operatives shrugged more deeply into their gray coats, looked around furtively, and melted into the mist. Only McHammer remained.

"Unc, uh, sir?" he said softly. "Getting in touch with you only through Contacts is so, uh, cumbersome. If I could talk to you alone from time to time as, uh, we— You know I wish to advance in the organization! If I can be helpful—a special assignment now and then— Sir?"

He peered into the drifting fog.

There was no reply.

The briefcase had disappeared from the ground.

McHammer stood alone under the bridge. And the gray fog swirled around him.

THE NEXT FEW DAYS were taken up with everybody at the big, old house getting used to everybody
else.

The Blackpools had to get used to Dilly's unexpected comings and goings on his bicycle. But he
tried to remember to keep them informed. And he
was never late for meals.

Dilly, in turn, had to get used to the Blackpools,
to their curiosity about his whereabouts, to Mrs.
Blackpool's skitteriness—she always looked as though
she had just spied a mouse—and to Blackpool's quiet
ways. Blackpool had the unnerving habit of turning
up silently in one room or another. He would make
his presence known with a question or a comment.
Dilly sometimes wondered exactly how long Blackpool had been there, watching him, before he spoke.
It was unsettling.

And then the Blackpools and Dilly and Contrary
all had to get used to each other.

Mrs. Blackpool was twitchy about dogs. "Nice dog," she would say, flapping her apron. "Now you just run off and play." Which only made Contrary go to her and nose at her shoes.

She didn't understand at all when Dilly would say, "Atta boy, Contrary, that's right—you go to Mrs. Blackpool now and tell her how much you like her."

Mrs. Blackpool's expression would change from desperation at Contrary's friendliness to annoyance with Dilly for encouraging all that unwanted affection, and then to bewilderment when Contrary turned away and went back to Dilly.

As for Blackpool and Contrary, it was strictly hands off. They eyed each other coolly and kept their distance. Each, for the other, was simply not there.

To give him credit, Blackpool did see to it that there was a water dish in the pantry. And food for Contrary turned up at every meal in the dining room alcove.

Eating with Contrary munching away beside the table was pleasant. Dilly lost some of that feeling of being a leftover boy, stranded at school between terms.

Watching television upstairs in the den after dinner in the evening, Dilly often found Contrary's eyes fixed on him. He would drop a hand to Contrary's head, and Contrary's eyes would close in contentment. Dilly felt a special kind of contentment, too.

Contrary showed no inclination to go back to Noah Jones's Ark. He just took naturally to lolloping along beside Dilly, whether on jaunts around Hennessy Depot or out into the surrounding hills. The only times Dilly had to go into reverse—to tell Contrary firmly to go instead of come—were when Contrary's curiosity was roused by something, or when a rabbit challenged him to a chase, or when Mrs. Blackpool was around. Contrary did seem to like Mrs. Blackpool.

"He's always under my feet," she sighed one morning as she stepped around the kitchen, making a picnic lunch. "I'm afraid someday I'll spill something hot on him."

"Hear that, Con boy?" asked Dilly, pointing to Mrs. Blackpool. "You just keep on showing Mrs. Blackpool how much you like her."

Contrary trotted to the door and stood waiting, looking back at Dilly.

"And I'll never understand those mixed-up directions you give him," Mrs. Blackpool said resignedly.

Dilly stowed the lunch in his backpack. "We'll get out from under your feet, ma'am." He slung the backpack onto his shoulders. "We'll be gone most of the day."

"Where do you go when you disappear for the day?" she asked. "Hennessy Depot isn't all that big."

"I put more than twenty miles on my bike yesterday." Dilly laughed. "All of them straight up or straight down. This sure is hilly country."

"Well, you be careful now," she cautioned. "And don't be late for—"

"Dinner," finished Dilly. "I won't."

Contrary was leaping at the door, making low noises deep in his throat.

"Looks to me like you really don't want to go somewhere, boy," Dilly said to him. "Well, if that's the way you feel, we won't go." He opened the door. Contrary shot out into the sunshine. Grinning, Dilly ran after him.

DILLY SAT WITH HIS BACK against an angled tree trunk. He had finished his sandwiches and was eating an apple. Nearby, a stream splashed over mossy stones. An occasional chip of gold flecked the water, cast there by an errant sunbeam cutting through the trees. Ground-hugging plants spread out around him in carefree tousle.

His bike leaned against a tree. Contrary lay beside him, gnawing hollowly on a bone.

"You know, Con," said Dilly, "I've got this secret. I haven't ever told anybody."

Contrary seemed to know Dilly was talking to him. He looked up from the bone, his eyes bright.

Dilly finished his apple, poked a hole in the ground, dropped the core into it, and patted the earth over it. "There isn't anyone around here, not for miles. Nobody can hear if I tell you."

Contrary cocked his head. He seemed to agree that they were a long way from civilization.

"It's this," said Dilly. He reached into his backpack and took out his pocketknife. He placed it on the ground, held his hand well above it, and relaxed. His hand tingled. The pocketknife lifted and smacked into his palm.

Contrary let out a surprised yelp. Something out of the ordinary was going on here.

"That's something, huh?" said Dilly. "It's a talent, I guess. The thing is, I don't know what to do with it. Even if you've got talent, you have to practice to make it better. Athletes do. So do musicians."

Contrary rested his nose on his paws, the bone forgotten, attending to Dilly's words.

"My father told me he was going to help me learn about it. But then he and my mother were —" Dilly didn't say the word. "So I guess it's up to me to find out whatever it was my father was going to teach me."

"Ah-oooo," Contrary moaned softly. He inched closer to Dilly.

"But I don't guess I should do this where anyone can see me," Dilly went on. "It sure would cause an uproar. So, where do I practice? And what do I do for practice? And when I get better at this, what good is it?"

He toyed with the pocketknife, playing with it, placing it on the ground and then letting it rise into his hand.

"So," said Dilly, "you can't seem to learn many tricks, Con. And I don't know what to do with the tricks I can do."

He put the pocketknife back into his backpack and took out a couple of dog biscuits. "And that's my secret, Con. Don't tell anyone, huh?"

Dilly held up one of the biscuits. "Say 'please'?"

But Contrary didn't say please. He just didn't get the idea, even when Dilly told him not to say please. When Dilly could no longer ignore the pleading eyes, he gave the biscuits to him anyway. "I'm not supposed to do that when you get things all wrong. But I don't care. You're okay, Con."

Contrary crunched up the dog biscuits. Then he picked up his bone and went to bury it beside the stream.

Dilly pulled off his shoes and waded through the stream. The cold wetness bubbled around his ankles. On the far bank, he sat on a rock and put his shoes back on. Contrary still lay on the grass near his buried bone, watching Dilly.

"You coming?" called Dilly. "Or are you just gonna sit there guarding your bone? Well, wait for me, then." He stood and started through the trees. "Or go on home without me," he called, pointing.

Contrary sounded his deep bark and splashed through the water. Dilly laughed and pushed on through the brush.

He was midway up one of the hills that surrounded Hennessy Depot. Away from the road, trees blocked out the sunlight. Underfoot, a tangle of vines and low growth made walking difficult. Rotting logs lay where they had fallen long ago. Here and there a dead tree leaned at an angle against another tree. The woods looked as though no human foot had ever touched the ground.

Contrary caught up with Dilly and passed him, bounding on his short legs through the underbrush.

"Where you going, boy?" called Dilly.

With a *whirrr* and a *chuck-chuck-chuck*, a bird rose out of the ground cover and flashed away on bright wings. Contrary gave out a belling cry and streaked after it.

"Con, you leave that bird alone," yelled Dilly. "I mean, follow that bird! See if I care."

Contrary ignored him.

Dilly ran stumbling over the uneven ground, his feet plunging into unexpected pockets in the earth. Contrary was quickly out of sight, but his voice told Dilly where he was. Suddenly the familiar "ah-oooo" gave way to excited barks.

Dilly burst through the greenery and saw Contrary. He was leaping at a fence. The bird had come to earth some distance beyond, inside the fence.

"Calm down, boy," Dilly said, laughing. "Face it! That bird just outsmarted you!"

Soothed by Dilly's voice, Contrary grew quiet.

But—what was a fence doing here in the woods? It was a this-means-business kind of fence, high and topped with barbed wire angled outward, a fence definitely meant to keep people out.

With Contrary at his heels, Dilly followed the fence for some distance in both directions. But he didn't see an end to it. Somehow, rambling in the woods lost a lot of appeal with a fence beside you, and at last Dilly turned back to the stream and his bicycle.

Riding down the hill toward town, he turned at a side road. He had noticed it on his way up the hill and filed it away in his mind for later exploration. He rode carefully, watchful of rocks and ruts. This was not what would be called an improved thoroughfare.

In time, the road brought him to what he half-expected to find—a fence set back among the trees. He stopped, inspecting it. Yes, it was the same sort of fence he had discovered higher up, in the woods.

He rode on, slowly, peering inside the enclosed area. He saw nothing but trees. Maybe it was some kind of private nature preserve.

He wasn't surprised when he came to a gate and found it closed. He dropped a foot to the road, staring into the compound. But he didn't see anything that looked like a house or a building. Nor did he see the scanning camera concealed high in a tree, aimed at the gate.

Dilly turned and headed back to the main road, back to Hennessy Depot, feeling good with the late summer sun warm on his face and arms. "We've had a good day, Con," he said. He sighed. "It'll be our last ramble for at least a week, you know. School starts tomorrow."

School. Public school. He wondered what it would be like to go to public school.

"*AND THEN WE CAMPED* at Porcupine Ridge State Park."

The first day of school. The day everyone said his name and what he had done during the summer. How many times had Dilly stood up in strange class-rooms and told about himself!

"Someone said he saw a UFO," the boy in the purple sweatshirt went on. "I got up during the night for three nights running to check it out, and my mom got really mad at me. But I didn't see anything," he finished in disappointed tones.

Questions tumbled from the class. "Wow! Weren't you scared?" "Were you alone?" "What if these little guys with skinny legs and great big heads got out of this spaceship and —"

"Hold it," called the teacher, Mr. Kennedy. "The fact is, Bryan didn't see a UFO. When he does, you can ask questions. How about you, Jessica? Do you want to share your summer experiences with the class?"

Dilly studied the girl who stood up. She had long dark hair and eyes the color of cornflowers and a way of tilting her head down and looking up out of those astonishing eyes. She was the daintiest girl Dilly had ever seen. But then he hadn't seen many girls. His schools had all been boys-only.

"We didn't take a vacation together because summer's the construction season and my dad's always busy then. But I flew to California to see my grandmother." She smiled and her braces flashed. "I went all by myself." She sat down.

"Dill—" Mr. Kennedy started to say.

A sandy-haired boy, Matt, interrupted. "She didn't tell the best part. She didn't say what she got for her birthday."

"Jessica?" Mr. Kennedy asked. "Do you want to tell?"

The girl squirmed and looked down. Her hair fell forward like a curtain and hid her face.

"Aw, come on, Jess," said the boy.

She looked embarrassed. "Most of you know what I got."

But not everybody did. "Tell, tell!" they clamored.

"Well, I got a"—she blushed—"a bulldozer."

"A *real* one?" asked someone. "Not a toy?"

"Real," said Jessica. "My dad says he'll rent it out to anyone who needs a bulldozer and put the money in my college fund. He says it's mine, only I don't feel like it is. I mean, it'll be lots of years before I can even drive a car!"

"I can drive, all right," said the sandy-haired boy. "I've been driving tractors around the farm since I was eight. But I don't own one. Wow!" he said in awe.

Dilly was impressed, too. By the boy—imagine knowing how to drive a tractor! And by the girl—imagine pointing to a bulldozer crawling around a construction job and saying, "That's mine."

"Dilloway McBean," said Mr. Kennedy, checking Dilly's name on his class list and looking up to meet his eyes. "Welcome to Ida Bertha Hennessy Community School. Do you want to tell us a little about yourself?"

Dilly pried himself out of his seat.

"Call me Dilly," he said, looking around at the interested faces turned to him. All these kids knew each other. He was the only stranger in the class. "I was in boarding school. But I'm here for—" He stopped himself. He had almost said "for this year." He changed it. "I live here now."

Mr. Kennedy tried to help him along. "Any special interests, Dilly? A favorite sport? A pet?"

How could he have forgotten good old Contrary. "I've got a dog. His name's—"

The bell cut through his words. Instantly the room was filled with the sound of books slammed shut, of talk and laughter.

"All right now, everyone," Mr. Kennedy called over the hubbub. "Be sure you know where you're going for your next hour. And someone point Dilly McBean in the right direction. Give him a hand today, until he knows his way around the building."

Dilly tucked his notebook under his arm, checked his class schedule, and headed for the door.

"Where you going next?" asked a voice beside him. It was the boy in the purple sweatshirt, Bryan.

Dilly showed him his class schedule. "It says here General Science."

"Hey, Jess," Bryan called. "Dilly's going to Gen Sci. Why don't you let him walk with you? See you around," he said to Dilly and pushed past some kids and disappeared in the milling crowd.

Jessica looked at him shyly. "We go this way."

Dilly fell in beside her, wondering what he was going to talk to her about. He didn't know how to talk to girls.

"What's your dog's name?" she asked.

Dilly told her and explained about Contrary.

She laughed. "You could've called him Wrong

Way Corrigan. We learned about him in Social Science last year. He flew the wrong way and ended up in Ireland." She turned at a doorway. "This is Gen Sci. 'Bye." She went to sit with a group of girls.

Dilly found a seat near the back of the room and waited for class to begin. Then it hit him that he had just talked to a girl—and it wasn't hard at all. He glanced toward Jessica. She was looking at him. She smiled a crooked little smile, her upper lip held stiffly over the braces, then dropped her eyes.

He had talked to her just the way he talked to boys! Well, maybe she had made it easy for him, asking about Contrary.

The teacher's name was printed on the board. Miss Pritchard. She started talking even before the class bell rang. Everyone had to quiet down to hear her.

"—year class participates in the statewide science fair," she was saying. "Your projects will be a big part of your work in this class. Choose something that particularly interests you. Then make up an experiment that shows what you . . ."

Magnetism. He would do a magnetism project. He probably knew more about magnetism than any kid in the whole world.

"Now in addition to your projects," Miss Pritchard continued, "we'll look into the various fields of science. Since this is General Science, we'll study a little botany, a little biology. We'll work with microscopes for the first time, seeing things the naked eye cannot see. And—"

Yes, thought Dilly. He was going to like this class. Science was his favorite subject, and nothing he was hearing sounded much different from other such classes he had been in. He already knew about microscopes, but he wouldn't mention that. He didn't want to seem too different from the other kids. And anyway, he knew he would have to work extra hard in some other class. Maybe in Social Science. Who was that Wrong Way Somebody-or-other Jessica had talked about?

When the bell rang, Jessica pointed him toward Language Arts. Matt, the sandy-haired boy who could drive a tractor, waved to him and they sat together. Later, he found that Bryan was in his math class. And they all—Dilly and Bryan and Matt and Jessica—ate lunch in the cafeteria together. It was during lunch that he decided it was the kids, not the classes, who made the Ida Bertha Hennessy Community School different from all the others he had attended.

Matt lived on a dairy farm outside the town. Bryan's dad was the editor of the *Tri-County Record*, the newspaper. Jessica's father owned a construction company and her mother worked at the bank. They talked about basketball and the harvest festival and Bryan's mom being in a play, just as the kids in the other schools had done. The difference was, the basketball game and the harvest festival and the play were all right here in Hennessy Depot, not in New York where someone's dad was a stockbroker and got tickets for all the pro games, or in London where someone else's mother was starring in a play. And when they talked about going home, these kids meant today, after school, not home for the Thanksgiving or Christmas holidays.

By the time he headed for his bicycle that afternoon, Dilly could find his way around school and had a start on knowing some of the kids. It wasn't going to be hard to settle in at the Ida B.

He unlocked his bike from the rack and headed around the side of the school and onto the drive that led to the street. That's when he saw Blackpool. The long black car was parked halfway down the street under some trees. Blackpool was just sitting there, watching the school and the yellow buses lined up in front of it.

Had Blackpool been sitting there all day, just waiting for him to get out of school?

Something clicked in Dilly's mind. Yesterday, out in the farm country that ringed Hennessy Depot, had he seen the black car moving slowly in the distance? Certainly he hadn't seen it higher up, in the hills. But down around the town where traffic was heavier? He rubbed his forehead, trying to recall. Perhaps he had, without letting the fact really register in his mind. But he couldn't be sure.

Well, he could certainly keep an eye open in the future. As for now— I wonder, thought Dilly. I wonder what he'll do when I head for home.

There was only one way to find out.

He rolled down the drive and turned into the street. He rode for a block, two blocks, three, then looked back over his shoulder. The black car was nowhere in sight.

THE BUSINESS DAY had almost come to a close at the Commercial Chemical & Corn Trust & Savings Bank. Jepson Whirtby gathered up a pad of yellow paper and several well-sharpened pencils and strolled out of his office. "I have a, uh, meeting now," he said to the secretary of the department. "Please take my calls."

Jepson Whirtby got few calls. But he was practicing for the day when he would be important and calls would come for him whenever he left his office.

In the hall, he turned purposefully and made his way to the lower level of the bank and the safety deposit vaults there. He spoke to the woman in charge. "Has Mr. Orbed arrived yet?"

The woman smiled pleasantly. "He's been here most of the afternoon."

"I'll join him," Jepson Whirtby said briskly. "Whirtby's the name, J.B. Whirtby."

The woman scanned a card from the box on her desk. "Whirtby, did you say? Nobody by that name is authorized to enter the McBean vault."

Jepson Whirtby drew himself up. "I have been assigned by this bank to assist Mr. Orbed in matters having to do with the McBean estate," he said huffily. "I'm sure he is expecting me."

"I'm sorry," said the woman. "He didn't leave instructions that anyone was to be admitted. You can wait here for him if you like." She motioned toward a chair.

Whirtby leaned over her desk to see the card she held. "Er, uh, what names are listed for admittance?"

The woman whisked the card out of his line of vision. "That is confidential information, not to be given out. Young man, you should know better than to ask!"

Whirtby shifted uneasily. "I'm sure Mr. Orbed will be most disappointed that you wouldn't permit me to help him. You may tell him that I will be in my office. If I'm busy," he added over his shoulder as he turned away, "leave word with my, uh, secretary."

Crestfallen, he left the vault area.

The massive metal door of the McBean vault was closed. Inside, Homer Orbed sat at a table, reading. The only sound was the soft rush of air from the intakes overhead.

The room was lined with file cabinets. Some of the drawers were ajar. Folders from the files were spread out on the table. Mr. Orbed read with deep concentration, pausing now and then to reread, tracing slowly with his finger, his forehead crinkled in puzzlement. Then he continued reading, only to stop again and enter figures on a calculator. Peering down at the instrument through the round, gold-framed spectacles, his lips formed an occasional silent word. Looking into the distance, a finger tapping his lips, he sat back and seemed to consider the figures. Then he went on reading.

He finished at last, closed a folder, and stacked it on the others. He contemplated the folders, rubbing his forehead. A long sigh escaped him. "This is . . . yes, this is quite beyond . . ." He didn't finish.

AFTER THE FIRST DAY AT SCHOOL, Dilly kept a wary eye out for Blackpool. More than once, glancing out a window, he glimpsed the car cruising past the Ida B. That seemed to happen most often early in the morning, right after he arrived on his bike, or late in the day, when he was leaving.

Once, when he stopped for a malt at Shakem's, he caught sight of Blackpool at the drive-through pickup window. There was the car, with its unmistakable hood ornament. As it moved away, Dilly had a good view of Blackpool's thick-set neck and craggy profile.

And there were still those times at home. When Dilly did his homework in the library or watched TV in the den, he would become aware of Blackpool moving silently in the hall. He might come into the room to gather up the daily papers or set out a bowl of flowers. Blackpool always had a good reason for being there. And yet . . .

Dilly picked out Blackpool on the street now and then, too, when he'd gone to the park to watch a game or when he dropped in at the Big Wheel to put air in his tires. Hennessy Depot was a small town, and it wasn't surprising that people's paths crossed. But even so, Dilly thought he saw a lot more of Blackpool than simple coincidence could account for.

Then, as Dilly had just about decided that Blackpool was not at all to be trusted, the man would do something unexpectedly nice.

There was the time Dilly came home in the rain. He slogged upstairs and got into dry clothes, then went down to the library with Contrary trailing after him. He found a book that had his mother's name in it, written in a tall, graceful hand. He liked finding books his parents had held. There was a bookmark at a poem, one about traveling among the stars. It was by William Wordsworth, with a date of 1798! Dilly was reading the poem, to find out what someone who lived that long ago could possibly say about space travel, when there was a sound at the door.

Blackpool entered, holding a small tray. "Thought you might be cold." He set a mug of steaming chocolate on the desk and, next to it, a plate of cookies—people cookies and a couple of the dog kind for Contrary.

Dilly blew on the chocolate and breathed in the

wonderful smell, noticing the bits of chocolate floating among the bubbles on the surface. His eyes followed Blackpool's gray-jacketed back as the man left the room on silent feet. Could someone who brought you hot chocolate because you might be cold—who even brought dog biscuits for a dog he didn't much like—could such a person mean trouble?

And then there was the day Blackpool was sweeping out the hearth in the library. "House is mighty quiet," he said, "with just you here all by yourself. Why don't you bring your friends home? The missus will be glad to whip up some snacks. Just let her know." He finished with the ashes and laid a fresh log on the andirons. "A little noise would make the place a sight more homey."

Would that suggestion come from a man who couldn't be trusted? It was all confusing.

Dilly did invite Matt and Jessica and Bryan home, and after that they took to dropping in quite naturally. With the stereo on high and everybody talking at once, the house was certainly less quiet.

Jepson Whirtby dropped in regularly, too. Dilly would come home in the afternoon and find him talking to the Blackpools. Whirtby would stop talking when Dilly came in. He would follow him to the library and ask if everything was okay, and was the house running to his satisfaction, and add that he hoped Dilly would say good things when Mr. Orbed visited.

"It's important to me personally that this work out well," he confided one day. "I want to advance professionally." He lowered his voice. "I fully intend to be a vice-president, somewhere, before I'm thirty."

He seemed to think thirty was young. To Dilly, thirty was practically old age.

One day Dilly came home to find the long, black limousine in the drive. That could only mean that Mr. Orbed was in the house, for Jepson Whirtby drove a rental car.

Dilly let himself in the front door. Contrary was waiting for him, setting up a great racket, as he always did.

"Miss me today, boy?" Dilly asked, kneeling. Contrary rolled onto his back, wiggling, and Dilly scratched his chest. "Have we got company, Con?" Dilly asked. "Have we?"

Contrary rolled to his feet and bounded into the library, barking. Dilly followed.

Mr. Orbed sat with his walking stick upright before him, his hands resting on the round gold knob. His eyes were fixed on a bowl of bronze and gold mums on the table. "Beautiful things, eh?" he said, without greeting.

Contrary rested his forepaws on Mr. Orbed's knee.

Mr. Orbed stroked the long ears. "Got yourself a dog," he said, looking up at Dilly. "And a bicycle, I understand. Those two things add up to good times, eh?"

"Yes, sir," said Dilly.

"Done some rambling out where the birds' nests are, have you, lad?"

The blue eyes behind the round gold spectacles were bright and inviting. Mr. Orbed really seemed to want to know what Dilly was doing. And so Dilly talked—more than he had talked to any adult, ever—about riding among the farms and hills around Hennessy Depot. "I've put three hundred fifty miles on my bike," he said proudly.

Mr. Orbed listened, smiling. "And school? Everything's working out well there, is it? Not too big a change from boarding school?"

A change, certainly. But with the question put to him that way, Dilly realized how good the change was. And he realized something else. He was more content than he had been in a long, long time. "I like it here in Hennessy Depot," he said. "I really like it."

"Good!" said Mr. Orbed, punctuating the word with a light thump of the gold-headed walking stick. "That's what I hoped to hear." He hiked himself to his feet, leaning on the walking stick. "Anything troublesome comes up, you'll let the Blackpools know about it, eh?"

Yes, there was something troublesome. But he could hardly let the Blackpools know about it! Should he tell Mr. Orbed about his suspicions of Blackpool? For a moment he toyed with the idea. But what exactly was there to tell? His suspicions were only that, suspicions. Dilly let the moment pass.

Mr. Orbed rested a hand on Dilly's shoulder as they walked toward the door. "Apply yourself to your studies, lad. There's a lot for us to learn."

Dilly watched the car move away down the drive. A lot for "us" to learn? That was a strange way of putting things. Oh, well. Maybe Mr. Orbed talked the way some teachers talked, first person plural: Have we finished our assignment, class? Shall we put away our books now? Are we ready for general assembly?

The change in schools wasn't really too bothersome. Dilly had, after all, made a career of changing schools. As he had suspected, he was behind everyone in some things and ahead of them in others. Science was still his favorite subject. And the day Dr. McEvoy arrived, he knew it was going to be like no other science class he had ever been in.

It was the day they were using their microscopes, looking for invisible life in pond water. The door opened and Mr. Bloom, the principal, came in. With him was one of the tallest women Dilly had ever seen. She was dressed in blue, her white hair caught up in a knob on top of her head. Curly wisps drifted around her face—not a beautiful face, with its too wide mouth. Dilly watched Mr. Bloom and Miss Pritchard talking with her at the front of the room.

So this was Dr. McEvoy. Miss Pritchard had told them about her at the beginning of class. Dr. McEvoy had won some big science award and was taking time off from her university teaching classes. She had come to Hennessy Depot—"Where it's quiet," Miss Pritchard said—to write a book. Dr. McEvoy had offered to talk to the science class, and Miss Pritchard thought she might be willing to give advice about their science fair projects. "We are much honored to have her visit our school," she said.

You'd expect someone who had won a big science prize to light up a room with importance. But Dr. McEvoy didn't. She just looked like a nice lady, a nice tall lady.

Mr. Bloom shook hands with Dr. McEvoy and went back to his office. Miss Pritchard tapped on her desk for attention.

"Class, I'd like you to meet Dr. McEvoy. I've told you about her. I wonder"—she turned to the woman—"if you'd say a few words to the class?"

"I have a better idea." Dr. McEvoy's voice was

resonant. It seemed to bounce off the walls. She swept the class with eyes that were penetrating, intelligent. There was a hint of humor in the look as well, as though she expected to laugh at something any minute. The "importance" light flashed on! This was someone you had to pay attention to. She smiled, and her cheeks creased into deep dimples, softening the wide mouth. "You all just keep on with your work. I'll wander about and get to know you."

A general rustling filled the room as everyone returned to work. Dilly looked into his microscope, saw a paramecium, and began drawing it in his notebook. Dr. McEvoy strolled among the tables, looking at drawings, asking a question here and there.

She stopped beside a girl who hunched over her notebook, drawing with great concentration.

"MMM-mm. What have we here?" she asked, touching the top of the page where the girl had written her name. "Priscilla? That's some drawing."

"It's a paramecium?" whispered Priscilla questioningly, her voice lifting.

Leaning on the table with one hand, Dr. McEvoy studied the drawing. "Is that what you really saw under your lens?"

"Miss Pritchard said to look for a slipper shape," whispered Priscilla, not quite answering the question.

"Well, yes," said Dr. McEvoy. "But I doubt she

meant one with a bow on the toe and a high heel." Laughter played around the wide mouth. She peered into the microscope, turning the knob, focusing it. She straightened. "Look for something like a footprint, Priscilla."

She moved on.

"Good," she murmured here and there. "Decided on your science fair project?" she asked as she examined a boy's sketch.

"A wind-powered generator," said the boy. "It'll make something happen—a light go on, or a bell ring."

"Nice idea," said Dr. McEvoy. "Alternative energy source. Very much your generation's problem."

After that some kids volunteered information about their projects. "A mouse in a maze." "A chicken learning to feed itself by pecking the right button." Other kids wanted to keep their projects secret and talked about them in low voices.

Dr. McEvoy stopped beside Dilly's seat. She ran a finger over his drawing and then under his name. "Dilloway McBean," she said slowly. "Good. I see that you found the nucleus in the paramecium. Have you seen the cilia?"

"Those little hairs around the outside? Sure," said Dilly. "I'll put them on last."

There was an explosive giggle behind him. "Hairy footprints," someone said, choking on it.

Dr. McEvoy ignored the laughter. She leaned over and picked up Dilly's hand. She spread the fingers and turned it palm upward.

Startled, Dilly looked up at her as she studied his hand, turning it from side to side.

After a moment she restored the pencil to his hand and closed his fingers around it. She patted the hand and put it back down on the notebook. "Well, Dilloway McBean," she said softly. "Any idea of what your science fair project will be?"

Dilly's head whirled. Something was happening here. Dr. McEvoy's words were about the science fair project. But wordlessly, touching his hand, she had seemed to be saying something else to him.

A lifetime of hiding his feelings helped Dilly now. He didn't give away his thoughts. "Magnetism," he said through lips that felt stiff. His voice was cool. "I guess I'll do something with magnetism."

"Excellent subject. Excellent." Dr. McEvoy's voice was equally cool. "It has long interested me. Let's talk sometime about your project, Dilloway McBean," she said, and moved on.

Dilly sat, stunned, his drawing forgotten. He was only vaguely aware of Dr. McEvoy talking to someone behind him. "A paramecium with toes? Oh, I don't think you really saw that kind of footprint."

He looked down at his hand, felt again the warm, strong fingers opening it, turning it, making a fist of it around his pencil. Nobody, nobody since his father, had ever said anything to him about magnetism. Nobody even knew he had magnetism.

He swung around and stared at the tall woman who dominated the classroom like a great big glowing sun. She had moved once more to Priscilla's side. She picked up the girl's drawing. "Now that's what I call a paramecium," she said approvingly.

Priscilla bounced in her seat. "I really did see it! It really was there in the water. I think I'll do something about pond life for my project."

"Good, Priscilla," said Dr. McEvoy. "Who knows? Perhaps you've found your special talent."

Priscilla glowed. Over her head, Dr. McEvoy's eyes, those penetrating eyes, met Dilly's.

*Later that day
in an abandoned warehouse . . .*

*the ancient hand-pulled elevator creaked upward
on its weary ropes. It clanked to a stop at the top
floor. The slatted wooden gate clattered upward,
and Master Operative Gorey stepped out. He
looked around, past the dust-moted light angling
in through the grimy windows. As he peered into
the gloom, figures detached themselves from the
shadows and moved forward.*

    "Operative O'Mallet here. Sir!"

    "Operative von Pfist reporting. Sir!"

    "Operative Blunt present. Sir!"

    *The low voices were further muted by the dank,
unmoving air.*

    *The master operative rubbed his hands. The
sound rasped in the silence. "And what do you
have for me? Blunt?"*

The operative handed him a bulky envelope. "My report, sir. It contains a list of the boy's former schools and camps, along with their written evaluations of him. I have found a source at his present school who made copies for me. The reports reveal nothing unusual. The boy is quiet, orderly, displays no unusual academic ability other than an interest in science. His intelligence is keen, however. He seems to have no special talents beyond the ordinary interests of a boy of his age. He was generally liked at his schools, but kept to himself. Something of a loner." He paused. "It's only a hunch, but something here doesn't quite add up. I can't put my finger on it. I will continue to observe."

"Excellent work, Blunt," said the master operative. "Perhaps the answer will reveal itself when information from all sources is processed. You have only pieces of the puzzle. When assembled with others, the larger picture will emerge. O'Mallet?"

O'Mallet, too, offered a thick envelope. "My report, sir. The boy rides a bicycle everywhere. There seem to be no limits on his freedom. Unusual for a young boy of means."

"Careless!" There was contempt in the master operative's voice.

"He is often in the company of two local boys and a girl. I have included their profiles in my report. He has acquired a dog and seems to have developed coded language for the animal— probably a boy's normal interest in codes. The dog may be an obstacle in picking up the boy, though."

"Fine, O'Mallet, fine! You are helping to fill in the picture." Master Operative Gorey showed his pleasure. He smiled, a rare occurrence. "Operative von Pfist, your report?"

The operative brought her notes close to her face in the dim light. "The floor plan of the house is enclosed with my report. The boy spends time in the library after dinner, studying, or in the upstairs den, apparently watching television. His bedroom is on the second floor on the southeast corner. The light goes on in his room at about nine-thirty and is turned off at ten o'clock. Mc-Hamm-, uh, Whirtby entered the house for two brief visits recently. Dates and time in my report. Not long ago there was another visitor to the house, an older man, Orbed by name. He may be the boy's guardian. I have not yet confirmed that."

"Strange," murmured the master operative. "McHammer did not mention the visit."

"Sir?" Operative von Pfist spoke earnestly. "Permit me to protest this McHammer. He's an amateur. He's dangerous. When amateurs mix with professionals, there is always—"

The master operative interrupted her. He did it smoothly. "Suitability is not for us to judge, my dear von Pfist. A greater intelligence than yours makes such decisions. You are simply among the gatherers."

"Sir!" Operative von Pfist's voice was sullen.

The master operative slid the reports into his briefcase. "I wish you to familiarize yourselves with patterns of action —the boy's, the household's, the school's. These will be needed if we decide to take him. A week from today, call Contacts for our next meeting. My feeling grows that this boy may be of singular use to us."

The operatives retreated into the shadows.

Master Operative Gorey turned up his collar, tugged his hat lower over his eyes, and entered the elevator. The rattling of the descending cage masked the squeaking of rats emerging from the walls of the old building to reclaim it from the intruders.

DILLY WANDERED AROUND HIS ROOM, thinking, thinking. It was the one place in the house
where he could be reasonably sure Blackpool would
not turn up unexpectedly. Especially when the door
was closed.

He flipped the switch on the sky lamp and absent-
mindedly watched the comets whiz around the globe.
He reached out and fingered the old red bowl that
had been Clyde Alexander's. Then he held his hand
above the bowl. His fingers tingled as he released
a magnetic pulse. Instantly the bowl smacked up
against his hand and stuck there. He lowered it to
the table and withdrew the pulse. The bowl remained where he placed it. Again he held his hand
above it, and again the bowl flicked up to his fingers.

Dilly only half-saw what he was doing. His mind
was on other things. An old scene was replaying
itself before his inner eyes. He felt his father's pres-

ence hunkered down beside him on the garden path on that day so long ago: This is a game your mother and I know about. But it's our secret, and now it's yours. . . . I'll be teaching you more about it. . . . Mustn't play these games in front of anyone . . . your word of honor . . . word of honor . . . word of honor . . .

But his father had not been expecting an accident. He had not been able to teach him about "the game," his magnetism.

Dilly looked down at his hand, toying with the old red bowl. The game, this talent he had—it wasn't of much use that he could see, except for doing tricks that would amaze people. And those tricks were worthless if you never had an audience.

There was something more. The talent had its drawbacks, too. He had always and forever to be aware of it, not to let the magnetism fly loose, unchecked. Control had become second nature to him. Only rarely did he forget, as had happened the day he arrived at the house and the engine of the train flew into his hand. But what would happen if someday he was startled or scared and completely forgot himself in front of a whole bunch of people?

He let the red bowl settle to the table and flung himself on his bed. He reached out and with a finger traced the constellation Orion on the lamp.

The bed bounced and Contrary landed beside

him. Dilly dropped a hand on the dog's head. "That's right, boy," he said. "Don't you lie on my bed." Good old Contrary. Dilly didn't feel quite so alone with Contrary right there next to him.

He wished he could talk to Contrary and that Contrary could answer back.

"Listen, boy," he said, somewhere deep in his mind. "This amazing thing happened at school. This lady came to science class and she seemed to know about me. She picked up my hand and looked at it. When I said I was going to do a project on magnetism, she said excellent and we'd talk about it. She said she was interested."

In the back reaches of Dilly's mind, Contrary seemed to answer. *Are you sure? Just because she picked up your hand? Just because she said she was interested in magnetism? After all, she was "interested" in all the kids' projects.*

"Well, no," Dilly admitted silently. "I'm not really sure. But I'm not *NOT* sure, either. She seemed to be inviting me to talk to her."

You may be making all of this up was the silent reply.

"If I talked to her"—Dilly's forehead wrinkled as he thought—"I'd be breaking my promise. I gave my word. I've never talked to anybody about magnetism."

Contrary gave Dilly's hand a swipe with his tongue.

It's important to be a man of your word. A man's got to stand for something.

Dilly sighed. "But since my dad can't teach me what he meant to teach me, maybe there's something I've got to learn."

Contrary opened his mouth in a prodigious yawn. *Maybe you should find out more about that lady.*

⊜

"*I HEARD MR. BLOOM TALKING* to Mr. Kennedy yesterday," said Jessica. "He said Dr. McEvoy's a really important person. He said one of her ideas set the scientific community—" She looked puzzled. "Sounds like scientists all live in one town. Anyway, set the scientific community on its ear."

Dilly, Bryan, and Jessica were riding partway home with Matt, and Dilly was following up on his resolve to find out more about Dr. McEvoy. All he had had to do was mention her name.

"My dad wants to interview her for the *Record*," said Bryan. "Maybe I can interview her for the *Ida Buzz*, too."

"She rented the old Hartrey place, near us," said Matt. "I wonder what kind of . . ." His voice faded. "Look!" he said in tones of reverence. "Which one is it, Jess?"

He had come to a stop near a construction job. A sign said that this was the future home of the Apex Iron and Brass Works under construction by Monroe Mackenzie, Contractor. Dilly, Bryan, and Jessica braked beside him.

Matt's eyes were fixed on a couple of bulldozers. Neither was moving. Work had stopped for the day. One of the big machines was mounted on a trailer, ready to be hauled to another job. The other stood near a mound of dirt.

"That one," said Jessica, pointing. "You can see it's newer than the one on the trailer."

Matt went to inspect the bulldozer. The others dropped their bicycles and followed him.

Matt walked around the machine, his eyes glazed. "Wow," he said softly. He reached up and stroked it. "Wow! You could move a mountain with this baby."

"Why would you want to?" Bryan asked reasonably.

Matt didn't reply. "How many cubic yards can it handle?" he asked Jessica.

Jessica dropped her eyes and shook her head. "Don't know."

Matt groaned. "This is wasted on you. You don't appreciate what you've got here."

"I know," Jessica agreed cheerfully. "But I'll find out for you."

"You're hopeless," Matt grumbled, heading back to his bicycle. "A real hopeless case."

They rode a bit farther with Matt, out beyond the

edge of town, where the houses thinned and farm-land began. Then Matt picked up speed. "I've gotta get home for chores," he called over his shoulder. "See you guys."

"See you," they shouted, watching him spin away down the center of the deserted road.

They turned, then, and headed back into town. Jessica declared that she was starved and wanted to go to the mall for a snack.

Bryan laughed. "A snack? For you that means three dogs and double fries."

Everybody teased Jessica about her appetite. She was as daintily made as a feather, yet she attacked food with an enthusiasm that put the rest of them to shame. She was good-natured about the teasing, though.

"Us delicate little types are pure steel inside," she said now. "We eat to keep up our strength."

Dilly rode with them as far as the mall. Then he went on to the Amy Frances Hennessy Public Library. There was still a lot he had to find out.

He told the librarian that he was looking for something, if there was anything, about Dr. McEvoy.

"The scientist who's here on sabbatical?" she asked. Hennessy Depot was small. Word about people spread fast. "Oh, I think *so*! She's written several books. We don't have them, but I can get them for you on inter-library loan. Here, this is a good reference."

The book she gave him was thick. It had reviews of books that had been published. He found several about Dr. McEvoy's books and was wading through them—the type was really small and hard to read —when the librarian came back. She laid a couple of old newsmagazines and a science magazine in front of him. "These might be useful," she said. "You must be doing an assignment for school."

"She sure is an interesting lady," said Dilly, not really answering her.

"Let me know if you want to get the books on inter-library loan," said the librarian.

The article in the science magazine wasn't easy to read, even a second time. But he decided that you had to be pretty important to write something so hard to understand and have a famous science magazine print it.

The newsmagazines were easier, and he learned a lot about Dr. McEvoy. She had been invited to the White House once. Her first name was Moira. It was funny to think about such a famous grown-up having a first name.

He stayed in the library until Blackpool came in.

The man didn't look at Dilly. He just checked out a book and left.

Dilly waited a while. Then he took the book and magazines back to the librarian. Somehow, he was glad Blackpool had not seen what he was reading.

Leaving the library, unlocking his bike, he saw no sign of Blackpool or the car.

That night, as he punched a comfortable place in his pillow and pulled the blankets around his shoulders, Dilly told Contrary, "I've found out as much about Dr. McEvoy as I think I'm going to. The teachers at school think she's great. I guess half the scientists in the country think so, too. She's written those books. They've written about her in those famous magazines . . ."

In the faint light from the sky lamp, Contrary looked up from his basket beside the bed. *So?* his eyes seemed to say. *So?*

DILLY TURNED IN AT THE DRIVE, dropped a foot to the gravel, and stopped. This was it, the old Hartrey place. He had passed it several times in his ramblings.

Contrary bounded ahead among the fallen leaves, sending up a whirlwind of russet and gold.

"Here, boy," Dilly called.

Contrary stopped and turned his mournful eyes on Dilly.

Dilly slapped his thigh. "Come on, Con."

Contrary came. Sometimes he did that lately, came on command, and sometimes not. Dilly never knew when he would respond. Maybe Contrary was learning, maybe he wasn't. He sat now, unmoving, at Dilly's feet while Dilly studied the house.

It was set far back from the road, half-hidden among the autumn gold of the trees. It looked like so many of the houses in Hennessy Depot, as though it had been built a long time ago, when people had a lot of time for sitting around on porches.

Getting here without being followed had taken some doing. That morning at breakfast he had off-handedly said he guessed he'd spend the morning at the library. Then, since it was Saturday, he guessed he'd ride around town. Matt and Bryan and Jessica might join him. They might go to the football game. Hennessy High was playing Washington High from over at Hickory.

He had said all that to Mrs. Blackpool, knowing full well that Blackpool was polishing silver in the butler's pantry right next to the dining room.

Would he be home for lunch?

Oh, they would all probably pick up something at the mall. He would call home at noon if Mrs. Blackpool wanted him to.

Leaving, he slung on his backpack, his notebook inside. Stopping in the kitchen, he made much of taking Contrary's leash from its hook near the door. "You're gonna have to wait outside the library, boy. I'll be in there for a while. Can't have you running loose." Then he whirled away down the drive, Contrary charging along at his side, heading for the center of town.

At the library, he locked his bicycle to the rack. "I'm going in there," he said, pointing at the door.

"Want to come?" Contrary lay down where he sat. "Thought that's what you'd say," said Dilly.

He clipped the leash to Contrary's collar and tied it to his bike. "Sorry, fella," he said. "I hate doing this to you." Contrary licked his hand. "With any luck, Blackpool will turn up soon now. Then we can take off."

He went inside, liking the old-house, old-book smell of the place, and found a book on mountain climbing. He carried it to a table near the tall front windows, where he had a good view of the street. He opened his notebook and got out his pen. Might as well make all this look like real studying, he figured. Then he settled down to read, keeping an eye on the street.

He had just got to high-altitude equipment when he felt a tap on his shoulder. Startled, he looked up, expecting to see Blackpool.

Standing over him, smiling genially, was Noah Jones, owner of the Ark.

"Well, m'boy," said Noah Jones. "I thought I recognized that queer dog parked out front. You didn't exercise your return privilege option, so I guess you two are getting along real well. Have you taught him any tricks?"

"Nope," said Dilly.

"Didn't think you would," said the man. "Well,

you can still bring him back if he's too big a dis-appointment. I've got a good Labrador pup out there at the Ark. Friendly animal. You two might hit it off."

Take Contrary back! The idea was so weird that Dilly laughed. "Contrary's okay," he said. "I won't be bringing him back."

Noah Jones smiled benevolently. "Well, the of-fer's an open one. Anytime. Anytime." He frowned. "Terrible thing to have a tender conscience. Hard to live with. But anyway, you stop in to see me sometime. Hear?"

"I hear," said Dilly. He watched Noah Jones head toward the stacks where the animal books were shelved. He sure is a friendly man, Dilly thought.

His glance swung to the window just in time to see the black car slow, pause, as Blackpool looked out at the bike with Contrary leashed to it. Then the car picked up speed and moved off down the street.

Dilly closed his notebook, stuffed it into his back-pack, and headed out the door. "Okay, Con," he said. "I think we're clear for a while. Let's go."

He unsnapped the leash, while Contrary shook himself. Then he unlocked his bike, swung onto it, and headed toward the edge of town. And now here he was at the old Hartrey place. Blackpool hadn't followed him. Nobody had seen him. He was free until noon.

The gravel crunched under his wheels as he pedaled slowly up the driveway, inspecting the house with its many windows. A cupola crowned the rounded, towerlike corner. A porch curved around the front and one side of the house. In back was a garage that looked as though it had once been a barn.

He rode around to the back of the house and leaned his bicycle against the porch where it couldn't be seen from the road.

What now? Should he just go up the steps and knock? What should he say? He had already made up his mind about one thing: He meant to tell as little about himself as possible while getting as much information as he could from Dr. McEvoy.

Even as he hesitated, the back door opened. Dr. McEvoy stood there. Her smile was direct, her words equally so. "Come in, Dilloway. I was hoping you'd drop in today." She stepped aside, making room for him to walk past her.

A faint whine distracted Dilly. He looked back. Contrary was sitting on the walk, his head cocked quizzically to one side, his eyes on Dilly.

"Uh, that's my dog, Contrary," Dilly said, by way

of introduction. "I guess I'd better leash him so he won't go and get lost while I'm indoors."

"Leash him! What kind of business is that for a friend! He's as welcome inside as you are. Come on, boy," she said, speaking to Contrary in the resonant tones Dilly remembered. "Come in and make yourself comfortable."

Contrary sat, his tail moving rhythmically from side to side.

Dilly patted his thigh. "Come, Contrary," he called.

And still Contrary didn't move.

Dilly put one hand on his hip, pointed back toward town with the other, and spoke firmly. "Now listen to me, Con. You are not to come into this house. Hear me? You can just go back the way we came!"

"Oh, but I—" Dr. McEvoy started to say.

Contrary picked himself up, ran-hopped up the steps awkwardly on his stubby legs, and marched past Dr. McEvoy and into the house.

There was a moment of bewildered silence. Then Dr. McEvoy threw back her head and shouted with laughter. She followed Dilly into the kitchen, mopping her eyes. "That's a unique system of commands, but if it's what he's used to . . ." She left the sentence unfinished.

She took a bowl from a cupboard, filled it with

water, and set it on the floor. "I'm putting this here so you won't drink from it, Contrary," she said, chuckling.

Contrary sniffed the bowl and then lapped thirstily.

"Would you like to not have some orange juice?" Dr. McEvoy asked, turning to Dilly.

He laughed. "Don't mind if I don't."

She poured a tall glassful and set it on the table. Then she pulled out a chair and sat down. Sitting, she didn't quite dominate the room as she did when she was standing. She poured a cup of tea from the pot on the table.

Dilly sat down across from her. He tasted the orange juice. It was cool and sweet and delicious. He took a long swallow and waited, not speaking.

"Your project on magnetism for the science fair is an exciting one," said Dr. McEvoy, fixing him with a look that seemed to cut right into his thoughts.

"I guess magnetism interests just about everybody," said Dilly, renewing his promise to himself to say as little about himself as possible.

"But especially you," she went on. Her voice softened. "As it should." She leaned across the table and gathered his hands into hers. "Ah, Dilloway, your magnetism is a great gift."

Dilly went cold. He pulled his hands away and wrapped them around his orange juice glass. "What do you know about me?" he demanded. "What do you think you know?"

"I know," she said gently, "that you possess to an extraordinary degree the magnetic force that exists in minute degrees in all of us."

Dilly didn't agree or disagree. "But how do you know about me?"

Dr. McEvoy's tea sat before her, untouched. "Mr. Orbed asked me to come to Hennessy Depot to—"

"Mr. Orbed! You know Mr. Orbed?" Dilly felt as though the breath had been knocked out of him. If Dr. McEvoy knew Mr. Orbed, perhaps— "Did you know my mother and father, too," he demanded.

Dr. McEvoy shook her head. "I never had that pleasure. I knew your father only through his published articles. I would have liked to know him. His thinking was highly original."

Dilly's thoughts were in turmoil. "But if Mr. Orbed knows about my magnetism, why didn't he talk to me about it? Why didn't he tell me about you?"

Dr. McEvoy's gaze was level. She wasn't smiling. She wasn't trying to charm him. "He didn't tell you about me because we didn't know when I'd be free for an extended period of time. My work, you know, and other commitments. Until I could make arrangements, Mr. Orbed felt there was no harm in just letting you enjoy yourself in a pleasant setting."

Dilly's mind was racing. The answer to one question only led to another. "But how did Mr. Orbed know about my magnetism?"

"You must ask him that," Dr. McEvoy said quietly. "I'm certain he will have answers to satisfy you. Try to be patient." She reached across the table and placed a warm hand on Dilly's. This time he didn't pull away from her touch.

The kitchen was still. The curtains on the window next to the table fluttered in a sudden breeze. The refrigerator hummed in the silence.

"I know this is difficult for you, Dilloway." Dr. McEvoy's voice was low. "You've been prudent in protecting your secret. That can't have been easy for a boy, and I admire you for it. But you're growing, and it's my guess that the magnetic force is becoming stronger. You can't continue to control it blindly, without full understanding of it. Only when you have explored it, when you have discovered what you can do—and what you dare not do—will you be truly in control. But to explore your gift, you need guidance. And that's why I am here," she finished simply.

Dilly looked up at the clock. He had been in this kitchen for less than half an hour, and he was changed. A boy had walked in the door. All that boy had had to do was keep cool, keep his magnetism under wraps, and he could just go on enjoying Hennessy Depot and his life there.

But he wasn't that boy any longer. Even if he never did anything about his magnetism, he now knew there was the possibility that he could. And that made him a different person.

"Suppose I don't want to be guided?" he asked. "What'll happen?"

"Nothing, perhaps," said Dr. McEvoy. "You'll just go on trying to keep your talent a secret."

"But maybe I'll forget, sometime," said Dilly. "Maybe I'll let it go without meaning to. What then?"

"Who's to say?" With a long finger, Dr. McEvoy traced the grain of the wood in the tabletop. "But to make a truly informed decision, it's probably a good idea to know everything you can about your gift."

Dilly thought about that for a minute. Then, "What did you mean, what I 'dare not do'?"

"I would guess you don't know the power of your magnetism. You don't know what unleashing it in its full strength could do to you. Might it weaken you or hurt you in some way we don't understand?"

That couldn't be! Or could it? The idea joined the others swirling around in Dilly's mind.

She continued softly. "If you wish, I will act as your guide. I will lead you, as it were, down a dark hall, doing my best to keep you from bumping into anything along the way. At the end of the hall there is light. By the time we reach it, you will know your capability."

Dilly was quiet, thinking. Then, "How do I know I can believe you?" he burst out. "I mean, why should I trust you? I know you're famous and all that, but—"

"Dilloway, look at me." Dr. McEvoy leaned across the table.

Dilly studied her face. It seemed a kind face. It was certainly an intelligent face. She didn't flinch or look away under his gaze.

"In taking charge of your life, you are going to have to develop your instinct about whom to trust or not to trust." Then she added briskly, "You don't have to make up your mind this instant. I've given you a lot to absorb this morning. You can think about it for a while."

Dilly sat, unmoving. Everything said in this kitchen this morning made some sort of sense. It was up to him to decide what to do about it.

In the silence, Contrary got up, crossed the room, his nails clicking on the floor, and went to Dr. McEvoy. He placed his forepaws on her chair and rested his muzzle on her knee for a brief moment. She stroked his head, looking down into his eyes.

Then Contrary came to Dilly. He lay down and rested his head on Dilly's foot.

At that moment, things fell into place.

There was no way he could find out for himself all the things his father had meant to teach him. Here was someone who could help him explore his talent.

He looked into Dr. McEvoy's face, her kind face. He didn't know it, but the look in his eyes was as penetrating as the look in hers.

"When do we start training?" he asked quietly.

DR. McEVOY'S FACE SOFTENED. She smiled, and the deep dimples appeared. "Now," she said simply. "That is, if you have a little more time to spare on this beautiful Saturday."

Dilly nodded. There was no point in waiting. He'd just keep wondering. "What are we going to do?" he asked.

"Nothing particularly dramatic to begin with." Dr. McEvoy stood up. "Let me get something from my desk. I'll be right back." She left the kitchen.

Dilly watched her go. I'm into it, he thought. Excitement bubbled around the idea. Since that day with the wagon, I've been waiting to find out more. And now it's here!

Dr. McEvoy returned and seated herself at the table. She opened a small carton and spilled paper clips before Dilly. She shuffled them about, then took his hand and held it above them.

"Now." She removed her hand. "Let's see what happens."

Dilly relaxed. His fingers tingled. Almost as one, the paper clips snapped up off the table and clung to his hand. They stayed there, sticking out every which way. Dilly grinned. "Just call me Porcupine Hand."

Dr. McEvoy's eyes sparkled. "Amazing!" she said softly. "Simply amazing!" Then, "But what happens now? Since you don't walk around with metal things stuck all over your hands, I gather you have a way of turning off the power."

"Uh-huh," said Dilly. "Simple." He let the magnetic pulse settle back into his hand. The paper clips tumbled, clicking softly, onto the polished wood. "It's like I'm one of those big electromagnets," he said, "dropping stuff in a junkyard."

Dr. McEvoy breathed deeply. "Simple it is not! Will you do that for me again? This time, don't release them."

Dilly repeated his performance. He was enjoying himself. For the first time in his life, he was showing someone what he could do.

Dr. McEvoy reached out and held his wrist, turning his hand this way and that. "Dilloway," she asked, her eyes fixed on the paper clips, "do you notice something here that differs from the usual magnetic pattern?"

Dilly studied his hand. But he could see nothing he didn't expect to see. He shook his head.

"The paper clips aren't clustered at two poles," she pointed out. "They're distributed pretty much uniformly on your hand."

So they were!

Bits of metal, such as the iron filings they used in science class, tended to cluster heavily at the two poles of a magnet. But the paper clips on his hand didn't do that.

"This tells us something about your magnetism," said Dr. McEvoy. "You create what is known as a uniform field over your entire hand. It's an interesting aspect of your magnetic phenomenon," she added thoughtfully, "most interesting. All right, you can release them now."

She watched as Dilly dropped the paper clips.

"Effective, your manner of letting things go," she murmured. "But it's somewhat—primitive, I guess I'd say. Possibly we can find a better release technique. That will come in time. For now," she went on briskly, "see if you can pick up a single paper clip with just one finger."

That was harder to do. All the paper clips jumped up onto his index finger at once, which wasn't what she had asked for. He looked up. "Porcupine Finger?" he asked.

Dr. McEvoy seemed pleased nevertheless. "You

were more successful than you know. You were able to direct the magnetic force into just that one finger. Try again."

Dilly kept trying. At last, clumsily, he lifted a single paper clip. "Got it!" he said triumphantly.

"Excellent!" Dr. McEvoy studied the paper clip that hung from his finger, attached at just one end. "Am I wrong, or are you releasing a weaker pulse?" she asked. "If it were stronger, the paper clip would be entirely magnetized and lie flat against your finger."

Only then did Dilly become aware that the magnetic hold on the paper clip was indeed delicate. "Hey!" he said. "I didn't know I could do that! I mean, I knew it, but I never thought about it."

"So!" Dr. McEvoy smiled. "We're learning together, Dilloway. Now, do you think you can do that with each finger, separately?"

Dilly worked on it. Sometimes he managed, with his middle finger. Sometimes not, and then the paper clips flew up and clustered on several fingers or on his entire hand. "This is really tough," he said, biting his lip in concentration.

"But you've got the idea." Dr. McEvoy nodded approvingly. "You're learning to fine-tune the magnetic force. Now I want you to practice doing that with each finger until you feel comfortable about it. Then we'll take the next step."

Dilly let the paper clips fall and Dr. McEvoy scooped them into the carton. "You can stop in to see me at school. Mr. Bloom has assigned me an office where I can meet with students to talk about their science-fair projects. You'll be just another student. Nobody will suspect anything unusual is going on."

Dilly leaned back in his chair and finished his orange juice. He set down the glass and studied Dr. McEvoy, his head tilted to one side. "Did you volunteer to help with the science fair because of me?" he asked.

Dr. McEvoy's sunny smile turned on. "Well, say ninety percent because of you. For the other ten percent, let's just say I enjoy being with young people."

She handed him the box of paper clips and he tucked it into his backpack. She walked with him to the door, her hand on his shoulder. "I'm glad you decided to trust me, Dilloway. I don't think you'll ever regret exploring your talent."

Dilly looked up at her. "Dr. Mac?" It seemed natural to call her that. "Thanks. Thanks a lot."

"*GO! GO! GO!* Hennessy De-poh . . . poh . . . poh!" The cheerleaders tumbled around in front of the bleachers.

Dilly, Jessica, Matt, and Bryan sat on the lowest

bench, with Contrary lying on the grass at their feet. Behind them, above them, sat the grown-ups— teachers and parents.

"Poppendick is the best quarterback we've ever had."

"Yeah, but look at the size of Hickory's linebackers."

"Ah, they're musclebound. Bet they can't run."

"Sure would hate to have one of them tackle me."

The talk swirled around Dilly, but he couldn't keep his mind on football. Not after the events of the morning. Dr. Mac's words kept surfacing, blanking out the game.

"Somewhat primitive, better release technique." What did that mean?

"What you dare not do." If, someday, he let out a terrific blast of magnetism, could he really hurt himself?

Ya-*hooooooo*! The crowd rose to its feet.

Dilly, still sitting, was suddenly surrounded by standing people. He felt as though he was at the bottom of a well. He looked around, up, confused, brought back to the present.

"Weren't you watching?" yelled Matt, turning and pounding him on the back. "Poppendick picked up twenty-five yards and a first down!"

"Who are we, we, we?" chanted the cheerleaders. They answered themselves. "We're the mighty Ida Bee!"

"Buzzzz," roared the crowd. Dilly joined them. "Buzzzz-zzzz!"

And still he could not keep his mind on the game.

Directing magnetism into one finger or another —funny he'd never thought of trying that. And using a weak pulse, controlling it at a very low level? Well, yes, he had known in a way that he could hold back on it. But the idea hadn't ever sat up and waved at him. Now he did know. Maybe he could handle the magnetism better.

His whole life had shifted and started off in a new direction this morning. In the light of that, football didn't seem very important.

Just when he thought the game would never end, it did.

"We won!" yelled Jessica, turning a cartwheel.

The crowd flowed out onto the field to surround the players. Contrary flowed with them, bounding, barking.

"Hey, Con," Dilly yelled. "Where do you think you're going?"

Contrary didn't even look back. Dilly ran after him. He stopped short when he saw Contrary skid to a stop and jump against Mrs. Blackpool's knees.

Mrs. Blackpool? What was Mrs. Blackpool doing at the game?

She petted Contrary gingerly, then brushed at him, trying to get him to stop jumping. "Nice dog. Oh, why do you insist on my attention?"

"Because he likes you, ma'am," said Dilly, approaching. "That's right, boy," he said to Contrary, "you just go on showing Mrs. Blackpool how you feel about her."

Contrary turned away and came to Dilly's side.

Mrs. Blackpool, looking exasperated, smoothed her skirt.

"I guess he was surprised to see you here, ma'am," said Dilly. He didn't add, But not half as surprised as I am.

"Oh, well," she said in her prim way, "it's such a pleasant day and all, I thought it would be nice to be out of doors. And I do have errands. I'll be getting along now, before the stores close."

She hurried away. Thoughtfully, Dilly watched her. Mrs. Blackpool and football? Who'd think that timid little lady liked football!

"Some game, wasn't it?" yelled Matt, coming up behind him.

"Let's go over to the Huddle," said Jessica. "I could eat a moose, medium-rare."

"Everyone in town was here," Bryan said, looking

around as they headed toward the street. "There's my dad. He covered the game for the paper. And look, there's Mr. Jones from the Ark."

And look, there's Blackpool, thought Dilly, as he caught a glimpse of the man moving along the edges of the crowd.

He wasn't even surprised to see Blackpool. He almost expected to see Blackpool wherever he went. He was reasonably sure he would see him at the Huddle in a few minutes.

And he did, out of the corner of his eye, as they turned onto the plaza. Then Blackpool was gone.

They decided to stay outside at one of the tables because of Contrary. Bryan and Matt, after teasing Jessica about her gigantic appetite, went inside for their orders.

Jessica watched them disappear into the building. Then she turned to Dilly, looking at him in that way she had, her head tilted down. "You're awfully quiet today," she said softly.

Dilly put on a goofy grin. "Forgot to turn on the bubble machine this morning, that's all."

She tugged Contrary up onto the bench beside her. "Come sit with me, boy." Contrary wriggled happily, and she sat with her arm around him. She was quiet for a moment, seeming to make up her mind about something. Then she looked at Dilly again. "I guess if something's bothering you, you haven't got anybody to talk to and that's got to be, well, strange. I mean, maybe you don't talk very much to the Blackpools."

She had guessed right about that one!

Rubbing under Contrary's collar, Jessica continued. "Well, you can talk about stuff to Bryan and Matt and me, you know, if you need ears. We're all friends. We think you're pretty neat." She looked up from under the veil of dark hair. Her eyes danced. "Except when you get Perfects on your math tests. Then you're obnoxious."

Dilly laughed. He felt a spreading glow, as though he was standing near a welcome fire on a chilly day. "Yeah, I do feel kind of quiet today," he admitted. "But there's nothing the matter. In fact, everything's great. I like living here in Hennessy Depot." He saw Matt and Bryan threading their way among the tables, balancing trays. "You know, I think you guys are neat, too. Except when you get one of your compositions back with 'Perfect—you write very well' written all over it."

Jessica giggled.

"Three for the Great Appetite," said Bryan, sliding a tray onto the table.

"Oink-oink," said Matt.

"You're just jealous," said Jessica, reaching for a

hot dog. She bit into it, then burped in a genteel way behind her upraised napkin.

They stayed at the Huddle until it was chore time for Matt and rake-the-leaves time for Bryan and babysitting time for Jessica. Dilly rode home thinking that friends were half of the best thing about living in Hennessy Depot. The other half was finding out about his magnetism.

That evening, he went to his room immediately after dinner. He closed the door and turned on the radio so that everything would seem normal should Blackpool walk down the hall outside. He thought for a moment, then went back to the door and turned the key. He didn't like the idea of Blackpool coming in and surprising him.

He folded himself down onto the floor, cross-legged, and emptied out the box of paper clips. Contrary lay across from him, his nose on his paws, his eyes on Dilly.

He worked until his eyelids grew heavy with fatigue. It was a slow and frustrating task, trying to pick up a paper clip with each finger. By the time he was ready to go to bed, he could do it with the index finger and little finger of his right hand and with the middle finger and ring finger of his left hand. His thumbs wouldn't cooperate at all.

He yawned and rubbed his eyes. "Maybe it's like

practicing the piano." He directed the thought at Contrary. "The more you practice, the better you get."

"Ah-oooo," Contrary moaned softly. He seemed to be agreeing with Dilly.

DILLY WOKE THE NEXT MORNING, caught in a dream. A giant paper clip was holding him in magnetic captivity. He was stuck to it. Weird. He shivered. But the dream didn't stop him from reaching for the box of paper clips and having another go at fine-tuning. He got his left thumb to pick up a paper clip before he went downstairs for breakfast.

He spent the better part of the day fooling with the problem—and becoming increasingly frustrated. His fingers just would not do what he wanted them to. If his right index finger worked, his left one didn't. He finally got both of them doing what he wanted, but then his left thumb went back to being uncooperative. He sighed and rolled his shoulders, which were beginning to ache.

Contrary, suddenly, seemed to have had enough of being cooped up in Dilly's room. He bounded to the door and barked.

"You've had it, huh?" said Dilly, returning the paper clips to their box. "I guess we both could use a little exercise."

He did a quick tour of the town on his bike with Contrary running beside him. Then he took them out River Road and on past the airport. He set a rapid pace, and when they neared home he felt good, his face tingling with the wind. He slowed when he saw the black limo parked in the drive.

Dilly's heart thumped. Answers. Answers were waiting for him.

Mr. Orbed was sitting in the back of the car. "Out rambling, were you?" he asked when Dilly opened the door to say hello. "Care to take another ride, this time with me?" His eyes, enlarged by his spectacles, had a soft shine to them.

"Let me put Contrary in the house first," said Dilly.

He let him in at the front door and Contrary skidded down the hall, ears flapping, heading for the kitchen and his water bowl.

Dilly went back to the car and settled beside Mr. Orbed, noticing that the glass behind the driver was closed today.

Mr. Orbed leaned forward and tapped on it with the gold head of his walking stick. They slid into motion.

"So you've met Dr. McEvoy," he said. "You've talked."

Dilly went straight to the heart of things. "She said you know about my magnetism. Did you always know about it, even when I was little and you let me see your watch that time? Wow," he added, "I could have ruined it if I'd let the magnetism fly."

"But you didn't," said Mr. Orbed. "You controlled it even then, small as you were. And, yes, I knew about your magnetism. But not the degree to which you possess it."

"Well, I guess I don't really know that either," said Dilly. ". . . What you dare not do . . ." Dr. McEvoy's words echoed at the back of his mind. He pushed them aside. There was so much he had to know. His head felt like a popcorn popper, with questions exploding in every direction. They burst out.

"Are there many people like me? I mean, magnetic? Dr. Mac said everyone has a little magnetism. But why do I have so much? And my parents, why did they? Is it something my father did in his laboratory? And what *use* is it!"

Mr. Orbed was calm under this barrage. "One at a time, eh? I'm fairly sure there are no other people like you."

"Then you aren't magnetic." Disappointment

sounded in Dilly's voice. He had rather hoped Mr. Orbed shared his gift.

Mr. Orbed shook his head. "I am not. My talents are of the more usual sort, but unique to me. I use them responsibly, in research. But getting back to your situation, I strongly suspect that your father induced the phenomenon. It may have been intentional. Or it may have been a laboratory accident."

He was quiet for long moments, his eyes fixed straight ahead. He seemed to be remembering. "I believe your father was going to tell me more about it. But that was not to be . . ." He continued briskly. "As to the beneficial uses of this extraordinary gift of yours? Ah, there's the challenge!"

So Mr. Orbed didn't have all the answers. Dilly's hopes of having everything neatly laid out before him evaporated. He felt like a balloon with some of the air let out.

Mr. Orbed's voice was kind. "We—you, Dr. McEvoy, I in whatever way I can help—are asking questions, making an intelligent search for answers. Things have a way of revealing themselves a little at a time when we do that. The bits add up, finally, and the answer emerges. Maybe we suspected all along what it was going to be. But at last we have proof!" The word came out forcefully, a kind of punctuation mark to everything he had been saying.

Dilly mulled that over, looking out the window

at fields of brown, standing corn brightened here and there with the cheering orange of pumpkins. Maybe "the bits" about his magnetism would "add up" someday. He had to believe they would.

But the questions about the magnetism itself were only part of what he wanted to know. There were other personal things.

He was tired of people sending him to schools and camps without asking how he felt about it. Of course, Mr. Orbed had talked to him about public school. He remembered being surprised about that. And he had liked Mr. Orbed for asking him. But still, Mr. Orbed had known way back then about the magnetism, and he hadn't said anything. So their conversations had been unevenly balanced, like the heavy kid sitting on one end of the teeter-totter while he, Dilly, was up in the air. Was that fair?

"Why didn't you say something about all this last summer?" he asked casually. He slid a hand into his pocket and brought out his pocketknife, turning his hand so that the knife hung suspended. "Or when you brought me here?"

"Astonishing!" Mr. Orbed's eyes were on the pocketknife. He plucked it from Dilly's hand, then let it flick back into place. He gestured to the car. "Is your hand drawn to the steel of the car when you do that? It must be."

"Well, sure," said Dilly. "I can feel the pull in a

dim sort of way. But the magnetism is weak. I guess if I let it out full blast, my hand would stick to the car."

He returned the knife to his pocket. "You could have talked to me when you brought me here to Hennessy Depot," he said.

Mr. Orbed sighed. He took off the gold-rimmed spectacles and rubbed his eyes. "Perhaps I should have. I'm sorry if that troubles you. I can only say that it seemed to me you had enough to get used to just then—new town, new way of life, new school, new people—without having to confront your magnetism as well. And then, I didn't know when Dr. McEvoy would be free to come here."

It made sense. But Dilly continued relentlessly. "Okay. But why now? Why this year? Why did you all of a sudden decide to bring me here?"

"Let me go back to the beginning." Mr. Orbed put the glasses back on. His eyes grew instantly larger behind them. "I was in Antarctica at a critical point in my research when the accident occurred. It was nearly a year before I got back to the States. By that time, you were settled in school. The bank's plan seemed sound. I expected to be out of the country for long periods, and you were safe, getting the care a small boy needs.

"Now you're old enough to begin working with

what you have. Hennessy Depot is a good place for you. It's off the beaten track. You won't come to much public notice. Dr. McEvoy can blend into the community. And it's a splendid place for a boy to enjoy himself." He gestured to the hills. "You need space for fun as well as work."

They had driven beyond farmland. The road ahead disappeared into forest growth. Mr. Orbed leaned forward and tapped the glass lightly. The driver nodded his understanding that they should head for home.

Mr. Orbed leaned back. "Your parents were, as the saying goes, dotty about you." He looked directly into Dilly's eyes. "They would highly approve of you if they could see you today."

Dilly liked knowing that. He felt warm. "My father must've been really smart," he said.

"Brilliant," said Mr. Orbed. "He had a grasp of scientific possibilities that I haven't met before or since. Scientists are still trying to comprehend fully, and prove, some of his theories."

As they neared town, home, Dilly remembered Blackpool. He swung around and looked out the rear window, half expecting to see him in the distance. But the only other car on the road was Noah Jones's van.

"Do the Blackpools know about me?" he asked.

Mr. Orbed shook his head. "They know only that you are a well-to-do lad whose home they supervise. Nothing more."

"Blackpool follows me," said Dilly. "He's always around, somewhere. Sometimes Mrs. Blackpool is, too."

Surprisingly, Mr. Orbed broke into laughter. "Either Blackpool isn't as skillful a tail as he thinks he is, or you're a lot more observant than he gives you credit for being. You weren't supposed to know. It's Blackpool's job to see that you're safe."

"A bodyguard!" exclaimed Dilly.

Mr. Orbed was still chuckling. "Oh, nothing so formal as all that. His instructions were to keep an eye on you. I'll ask him to ease up. This appears to be a safe enough environment."

Dilly began to laugh, too, thinking of how he had set Blackpool up to be outsmarted yesterday morning. He told Mr. Orbed about it. "But I won't do that anymore," he concluded, "now that I know why he keeps turning up places."

As they angled onto Josephine Street, Mr. Orbed thumped the floor lightly with his walking stick. "You are to be congratulated on your good sense in deciding to trust Dr. McEvoy. She's brilliant, you know. And a fine woman, a fine woman. Can't think of a better person to help you along."

"Except my father," said Dilly.

The car slowed and stopped before the house. "Except your father," agreed Mr. Orbed.

That night, Dilly lay on his bed, resting on one elbow. The paper clips were mounded in front of him. Idly, he dipped at them with the little finger of his right hand, trying to pick one up. Part of his mind was on what he was doing, part on the things he had learned that afternoon.

"I sure have learned a lot since yesterday morning, Con," he said silently. "Yesterday morning feels like a million years ago."

Contrary, stretched out on the foot of the bed, made a sound deep in his throat, as though in agreement.

"I wonder where it all will lead," said Dilly. "It's all an adventure. You never know what's gonna happen, with an adventure. They're full of surprises."

So surprise me! Contrary yawned. *Surprise me!*

JEPSON WHIRTBY WAS AT THE HOUSE the next afternoon when Dilly got home from school. Dilly kicked out the prop on his bicycle, left it standing in the drive outside the kitchen door, and went inside.

Whirtby was talking a mile a minute to the Blackpools. Blackpool was leaning against the sink, looking at him expressionlessly. Mrs. Blackpool, her head down, was stirring something in a bowl, her hand a blur of motion.

Stopping in midsentence, Whirtby turned to Dilly with his usual eagerness. "Well, here's our young friend, home from school. Time for a talk, old chap?" He turned back to Blackpool. "My man, perhaps you'd bring us a snack? We'll be in the library."

He dropped a hand onto Dilly's shoulder and steered him toward the hall. Dilly squirmed. For some reason, he didn't like Jepson Whirtby's hand on his shoulder.

An approaching racket in the hall, a scrabbling of feet on polished wood, announced Contrary's arrival. He burst through the swinging door. It hit Jepson Whirtby squarely on the stomach, thrusting him aside.

"*Oooof!*" Whirtby gasped.

"Ah-oooo," Contrary moaned soulfully, throwing himself at Dilly.

Dilly dropped to his knees to give him a good roughing up. "Miss me, Con?"

Contrary wriggled joyfully.

Dilly took a couple of dog cookies from the box on the counter. "Come on, boy, let's go see if you'll speak for these."

He led the way down the hall with Contrary jumping wildly around his feet.

Whirtby followed. He looked slightly bleary-eyed, but he smiled heartily nevertheless and tried to take charge of the conversation as they entered the library. "Things are going well, I understand."

Dilly hunkered down on the hearth rug and held up one of the dog cookies. "Okay, boy, what do you say?"

Contrary rolled onto his back, his paws in the air, playing dead.

Whirtby spoke to Dilly's back. "At least, that's what the Blackpools seem to think."

"Contrary, you cannot have this cookie," said Dilly, putting it with the others in his shirt pocket.

The reverse technique didn't work. Contrary rolled back over and looked longingly at Dilly's pocket.

"Aw, come on, Con, give it a try," said Dilly.

"I understand our mutual friend Mr. Orbed was here yesterday. You must have had a pleasant chat," said Jepson Whirtby.

So that's why Whirtby had come today! He was trying to find out if Dilly had said "good things"— as Whirtby had once put it—about him and about the house to Mr. Orbed.

Dilly could no longer hold out against the pleading gaze fixed on his pocket. "Okay, boy, you win another round," he said, digging out the cookies.

Contrary crunched them, making pleasingly hollow sounds. Dilly settled beside him. He sighed. Squirtby Whirtby just could not be ignored.

"I talked to his driver this morning. That's how I know he was here." Whirtby looked smug. "Have to keep up on things if I'm to anticipate Mr. Orbed's needs, to be indispensable, y'know."

Dilly didn't have to answer. Blackpool entered with a tray. He set mugs and plates on the low table.

"Thank you, my man," said Whirtby. "We appreciate this, don't we, old chap?" he said to Dilly, ignoring the stony expression on Blackpool's face. Blackpool did not, it was clear, like being called "my man."

Whirtby settled back in the wing chair and blew on his coffee. "I have a splendid plan. Why don't you and I"—he leaned forward conspiratorially— "go for a hike?"

Dilly stared at him, aghast. "It's too late. It gets dark earlier now." The absolute last thing in the world he wanted to do was go hiking with Jepson Whirtby.

"Oh, not today. I mean one day soon." Whirtby glowed with the inspiration of his plan. "Before the trees lose their leaves."

"Oh, but I—I—" stuttered Dilly, "I, uh, wouldn't want you to go to any trouble. I mean, you—"

"No trouble at all, chappie."

Dilly winced.

"I'd enjoy a good hike, the clear fresh air of the hills." Whirtby breathed deeply. "The autumn colors."

"But—but—" Dilly stumbled over the words, trying to think of a way out of this. "You don't have to take me hiking. I ride all over on my bike. And there's Matt and Jessica and Bryan—"

"Tut, old chap, tut!" Whirtby looked unusually

self-satisfied. "It's the least I can do. If Mr. Orbed can spend part of his weekend coming to see you, I'm sure I can spare a little time for you, too. Mr. Orbed will be pleased."

So that was it! Squirtby was setting up a hike to impress Mr. Orbed.

"I'll leave a message with Blackpool the day before I come." Whirtby set down his cup. "Oh, this will be jolly to look forward to!"

He left looking pleased with himself.

Dilly, looking anything but pleased, watched him go. He set his jaw. Squirtby might think they were going for a jolly little hike. Somehow, it wasn't going to happen. He pushed Jepson Whirtby out of his mind and went up to his room to practice with the paper clips.

In the days that followed, he worked hard at learning to "fine-tune." It was slow work. Sometimes he felt as though he was climbing a mountain, sliding back one step for every two he advanced upward. But his efforts were rewarded. With increasing confidence he learned to direct a magnetic pulse into each finger at will.

"You're becoming quite good at this," Dr. McEvoy said one day. They were in her office at school. "Now let's try for speed. I'll call them. You pick them up."

She spoke rapidly. "Left index finger. Right little finger. Right middle finger. Left thumb."

Nimbly, delicately, Dilly picked up a paper clip with each finger as she called it.

"Splendid!" she said softly. "You've taken enormous strides since that first day you tried this."

Dilly felt proud. He had worked hard.

"Tell me," she asked. "Have you been tempted to try putting out strong pulses?"

"Well, sure," said Dilly. "It's sort of like wondering how big a weight you can pick up. You just have to try, to find out. I'm curious. But I haven't done it. It's scary, not knowing what exactly might happen."

Dr. McEvoy nodded in understanding. "New territory usually is awe inspiring. We'll move ahead slowly. Then it won't be so scary." She nudged a stapler to the far end of the desk. "Show me what you can do with that."

Another step forward! He was moving beyond fine-tuning, beyond paper clips. At last! Now that he could control the magnetic output in each finger, work with the paper clips was becoming tedious.

He held out his hand. His fingers tingled with the energy they contained.

The stapler whizzed the length of the desk and smacked into his hand as solidly as a baseball slapping into a player's glove.

"Ouch!" Dilly dropped the stapler, surprised. He shook his hand. "That hurt!"

Dr. McEvoy took his hand in hers. She moved each finger, examined the palm on which a red mark was rising. She rubbed the hand briskly and continued to hold it as she spoke.

"Ah, Dilloway, I don't want you to be hurt. I didn't know that would happen. But it demonstrates the need for caution."

Dilly felt, suddenly, closer than he had felt to anyone since he was a little kid. It was kind of pleasant to have someone hold your hand, caring that it hurt. The warmth of the moment led him to talk of the thing that troubled him.

"Sometimes I wonder what would happen if I forgot and the magnetism just burst out. Anybody could see me."

"Have you ever forgotten?" She looked up from the hand she was still massaging. "Has it ever burst out, as you put it?"

"Sure." Dilly told her about some of his narrow escapes. "But most of the time I caught myself before anything really bad happened, or whoever saw something just didn't believe what he was seeing." He thought for a minute, remembering. "There was one time, though, when I made trouble and didn't even know I was doing it."

Dr. McEvoy patted his hand and put it back on the desk. Dilly flexed his fingers, inspecting the fading redness.

"We'd all just got to this computer camp and we were pretty excited. The instructor passed around a disk for us to look at, and I guess I got so interested I forgot to hang onto the magnetism. Anyway, when he put the disk into the computer, nothing happened. It was dead, empty, zilch."

Dr. McEvoy laughed. "I have an idea what had happened to it."

Dilly laughed, too. "That poor guy! There he was, showing us he knew everything in the world about computers and the first program didn't work."

"Did you know you had cleaned off the disk?" asked Dr. McEvoy.

"Not at first." Dilly shook his head. "I got the idea kind of slow. It took a couple of days. But you can bet I walked around the place on tiptoes the rest of that summer. I didn't forget about the magnetism again."

"I can see you've had your problems," said Dr. McEvoy. "The need for constant control has to be a strain on you, even though it's become a subconscious thing. I'm sure there's an answer. I'll"—she smiled—"help you worry about it."

Dilly felt—what? More calm? Less alone? Without putting a name to it, he knew things were just better with Dr. Mac tuned in on the problem.

"Now," she went on, "let's try the strength thing again, this time with something lighter than the stapler." She fumbled in the desk drawer, searching. "Ah. Here. This." She unfastened a large spring clip from a stack of papers. "And this time, let's begin with something already airborne. Ready? Less power this time."

She tossed the spring clip into the air.

The clip did not fall, as all things must. Instead, it swooped sideways and into Dilly's hand. It didn't hurt.

"Wonderful," she said softly. "You defy gravity, Dilloway. Now, set it down without dropping it."

"Well, it has to drop," Dilly explained. "I just let go. See?" He released it. The spring clip clattered to the desk.

"Good enough," said Dr. McEvoy. "But there's another way."

That was the day Dilly started learning to release objects gently, slowly withdrawing his magnetic grip.

*Some days later
high among the wooded hills . . .*

trench-coated figures were gathered in a long-forgotten graveyard. Shifting uneasily in the half light, they stood under the outstretched limb of a carved granite tree. The wind whistled. It sent curled leaves scudding among the tilting tombstones. Operative Blunt was speaking.

"A well-known scientist, a Dr. Moira McEvoy, visits the school regularly. Her profile is included in my report. The children are encouraged to confer with her regarding a science fair. The boy is frequently seen entering her office. He often waits at the end of the line of students and sees her last. He spends considerable time with her." Blunt was silent for a moment. When he spoke, puzzlement edged his words. "My intuition tells me something unusual is going on here. I have learned not to ignore my intuition."

Master Operative Gorey gave a single brisk nod. "You are right. Intuition plays an important part in our work. Stay with it, then." He turned to Operative O'Mallet.

"I have established a relationship with an excellent source." O'Mallet spoke rapidly. "Through him I learned that the boy visited the home of the scientist on a recent Saturday morning. He has not repeated the visit. The boy's guardian, a Homer Orbed, has called on him several times."

"Odd," Master Operative Gorey murmured to himself. "Je—McHammer has not so reported."

O'Mallet continued. "Most recently he took the boy for a ride. They went well beyond the town limits, driving for nearly an hour. I have not as yet been able to ascertain the content of their conversation.

"Orbed is a scientist. In recent years he has spent long periods at the South Pole. His research on penguins has been published in academic journals. The complete rundown is contained in my report. My intuition, too, suggests that things here do not add up. The man is small and what might be called portly. His manner of dress is rather dapper. These facts do not seem consistent with the image of a hardy type who spends months at a time in the polar wastes."

"So. We have mysteries here," the master operative said thoughtfully. "Perhaps Operative Mc-Hammer can be helpful in finding out more about Orbed. He may have access to his files."

"I beg your pardon, sir." Operative von Pfist was intense. "You speak of the importance of intuition. Listen to mine. This McHammer, this amateur—"

The master operative cut her off. "McHammer is new to operations. We must make allowances, use what he has to offer and hold him in check as seems called for."

"But the unexpected!" A chill wind rattled the dry grasses among the marble slabs. Operative von Pfist raised her voice to be heard. "The unexpected may throw our plans into chaos. If we start acting on the word of amateurs—"

The master operative did not let her finish. "My dear Olga, you are letting professional jealousy rule your head. Now let's get on with it. Your report, please."

"Sir!" Operative von Pfist read her report tonelessly. "The boy no longer spends part of his evenings in the den. The lights in his room go on directly after dinner. They remain on longer than formerly. Recently the boy and his friends rode their bicycles into the countryside. The boy led them to the compound and asked about it."

"They were observed," said the master operative.

"The girl could tell him only what is known in the town. That her father's company excavated part of the hillside for an unknown person or persons who planned to build a house. That the work was completed and paid for. That nothing more was done and a fence was placed around the site. That it has been abandoned in recent years."

"Excellent work, von Pfist," said the master operative.

"Thank you, sir." Operative von Pfist's voice was icy.

Master Operative Gorey placed the operatives' reports in his briefcase and snapped the lock. "We are close to our final action. Report daily to Contacts. You will be given a drop-off point for your reports. Be alert. Be prepared to act in the near future. We will now disperse in our usual clever manner."

"Sir!" "Sir!" "Sir!" The words were carried away on the wind as the operatives disappeared into the gloom.

Full darkness had descended. In the ebony night, an owl came to perch on the limb of the granite tree.

IN THE DAYS THAT FOLLOWED, Dilly saw less of Blackpool near school and around town. Mr. Orbed must have told the man to relax. Dilly relaxed, too. When he did happen to spot Blackpool in the distance, he didn't worry about it. And he didn't waste any more energy in trying to outwit him. He was free to think about the tasks Dr. McEvoy set for him.

He still worked with the paper clips. The fine-tuning exercises were a kind of warm-up for the other things he was trying to do. He had to improve on his release technique. He could see, now, that letting things just drop from his hands was pretty clumsy. And then there was the challenge of controlling the strength of the magnetic pulse, of attracting things without having them slam into his hands.

He had gathered together an interesting collection of metal things to work with. He thought of them as his "tools."

At first he had used a battered old pie plate and measuring cup from the kitchen. There were, he found, lots of small things in the kitchen that he could use.

He was forced to change his mind, though, the day he found Mrs. Blackpool wringing her hands. "My best pie plate," she wailed. "I can't find it anywhere. I need that particular pie plate for my lemon meringue pie."

Dilly took pity on her. Besides, her lemon meringue pie was a five-star event. He didn't care to think of a future without Mrs. Blackpool's lemon meringue pie!

Quietly, he slipped the pie plate and measuring cup back into the pantry and headed for Poppendick's hardware store.

Wandering through the aisles, he found himself among the camping equipment. A metal camper's plate, he decided, was far more interesting than a pie plate. And a camper's cup was much better than a measuring cup.

He was looking at a canteen, hefting it, feeling its weight, thinking that he could make it heavy or light depending on how much water he put in it, when Noah Jones stepped beside him.

"Planning a little camping trip, I see," he said.

His smile was broad, and Dilly thought again what a friendly man he was.

"Uh, not exactly." Dilly looked down at the things he held. They certainly did look as though he was going camping, and so he added, "Well, maybe one of these days."

"Pays to be ready." Noah Jones nodded wisely. "Never can tell when you'll want to spend a weekend in the hills." He picked up a canteen like the one Dilly held. "Had one of these when I was a boy. Carried it with me everywhere. Used to climb around these hills a lot."

It was hard to imagine Noah Jones as a boy, and harder still to imagine him climbing hills. It was, in fact, hard to imagine him doing anything more active than rocking in his chair at the back of the Ark.

Noah Jones looked thoughtful. "Now that I think of it, I may still have that old canteen and some other gear. Stop out at the Ark and I'll make a gift of it to you."

"Well, thanks," said Dilly, backing toward the checkout counter. Getting away from Noah Jones wasn't easy. He always wanted to talk when they met, and they seemed to meet often these days. "Nice to see you, sir."

"My pleasure," Noah Jones called after him. "Now you stop in to see me. Hear?"

Dilly didn't think that was going to happen soon.

He was too busy to go around visiting. He hardly had time to see Jessica and Matt and Bryan lately, and they were starting to complain about it.

Dilly put the canteen aside for the time being. He knew he wasn't ready for that yet. He worked with the plate and cup. The evening he managed, finally, to release the cup and it settled smoothly onto the table without clattering, he felt quietly proud. "Hey, Con, did you see that?" he asked.

Contrary opened one sleepy eye.

"You didn't," said Dilly. "Okay, I'll do it again. Now don't watch me."

This time, for the fun of it, he put a couple of jellybeans in the cup. Gently, slowly, he released it.

The cup wobbled. The jellybeans rolled noisily. Then the cup tilted, the jellybeans fell out, and it clanked onto the table upside down.

"Oh, well," said Dilly, "that just goes to show I'm not perfect." He grinned. "Yet."

Contrary ate the jellybeans.

Fine-tuning with the paper clips and learning to set things down easily was work. But testing his ability to attract things to himself was just plain fun.

"Hey, Con. Don't watch this," he said softly one evening as he prepared to pull a plate from the night stand beside his bed to the chair in which he sat near the door.

Contrary was worrying a bone. He looked up.

Dilly relaxed. He held out his hands. His fingers tingled as he released a gentle pulse.

The metal plate lifted momentarily, then thudded to the carpet in front of Contrary.

Contrary let out an alarmed yelp and laid a paw over his bone.

"Not enough power that time," muttered Dilly, setting the plate back on the table. He returned to his chair. "Hey, you better not watch this, boy."

Contrary watched, warily.

"Relax," Dilly said softly to himself, holding his hands out toward the plate. "Ready . . . set . . ." Again, the tingling. "Go!"

The plate moved away from the table, dipped, then lifted upward as Dilly strengthened the flow. The plate slid across the room and into his hands as neatly as a Frisbee.

"Great, huh?" he said. "I'm really learning."

Contrary got up, his bone in his mouth, and padded to the bed. He slid under it on his belly. A moment later, his nose and eyes appeared beneath the dust ruffle—and remained there. The bone was nowhere in sight.

"Aw, come on," said Dilly, laughing. "You didn't really think I'd take away your bone, did you?"

"Awww-rrr," said Contrary. It might have meant

"I know that." Nevertheless, he didn't bring out the bone again that evening.

Just as the magnetic thrust was sometimes too weak, it also burst out from time to time with unexpected force. One evening when that happened, static exploded from the radio. There was a tap on the door.

Startled, Dilly leaped soundlessly to unlock it. Then he dropped into the nearest chair, his eyes fixed on a book. "Yes?" he called.

The door opened and Blackpool looked in. "I heard something just now out in the hall. Was that your radio?"

"Yeah," said Dilly. "It made a terrific racket."

Blackpool crossed the room and fiddled with the volume control. The music went from loud to soft several times in rapid succession. "Funny," he said. "It seems all right now. I wonder if the missus was doing something with one of the appliances in the kitchen a while ago. I'll check with her."

He headed toward the door. "But if she wasn't" —he paused, his hand on the doorknob—"I'll take the radio to the fix-it shop to be looked over. I hope you can get along without it for a couple of days."

Dilly watched Blackpool leave. He couldn't help feeling guilty for putting him to unnecessary trouble. But there was no way he could tell the man he was positive the radio was okay.

Gingerly, rubbing the back of his pants, he got up from the chair. He looked down at the clutter of spoons, spring clips, and toy cars on which he had been sitting.

"The lesson of the day," he said silently to Contrary, "is: Only work with a couple of things at one time. And watch where you sit!"

Contrary got up and shook himself. *You're getting to be one smart kid* were the words that rose in Dilly's mind.

"I HAVE SOMETHING FOR YOU." Dr. McEvoy
dug into the pocket of the old blue cardigan she
favored and laid a watch on the desk before Dilly.

He picked it up, turning it in his hands. A present?
He never got presents! Whatever he needed or
wanted was always—just there. "Golly," he said.
"Thanks! Lots of the kids have watches like this. I'm
getting to fit in here more and more."

Dr. McEvoy was watching him closely. "It's more
than a watch," she said softly.

"It is?" Dilly looked up questioningly.

"To the casual observer," she said, "this is simply
an inexpensive wrist watch. But to you, it's a warning system. Whenever you emit a magnetic pulse,
you'll feel a vibration."

The meaning of the gift became clear. Dilly was
awed. "If I forget and the magnetism zaps out, the
watch will vibrate and warn me! I can turn off the
power before things happen."

He strapped it onto his wrist and released a weak magnetic pulse. Instantly the skin under the watch quickened.

Startled, he looked from the watch to Dr. McEvoy. "It really works! It feels like a buzz without any sound. It sort of tickles."

Dr. McEvoy laughed. "Well, I'm glad it works. The inventor would go into a decline if it didn't. He takes enormous pride in his work."

"You told someone about me?" Dilly was shocked.

She shook her head. "I told him only that I needed an instrument of this kind. Putting it into a wristwatch was his idea. But he couldn't understand"— she laughed softly—"why I wanted it on such a small wristband. He asked if I planned to wear it on my thumb."

Dilly glanced from his wrist to her hand and laughed. "I guess it would fit onto two of your fingers, anyway. I've never heard of anything like this," he added.

Dr. McEvoy leaned back in her chair. "There is no other like it. I know a great many talented people. The man who did this teaches advanced mathematics. He invents things as a hobby. Amazing individual."

Dilly remembered something. He looked at the watch again. "My gosh! It's still running! Why didn't it stop when I— I mean, watches get magnetized."

Dr. McEvoy shook her head. "This watch won't respond that way. It's shielded. In any case, if it does stop, the time-keeping portion can be easily replaced."

The full impact of Dr. McEvoy's gift hit Dilly. "I don't have to worry anymore about forgetting," he said in wonder.

"Not anymore," she echoed softly. "I believe the watch will help you to be more comfortable about yourself, Dilloway."

"Nobody has ever given me anything so special," said Dilly. Then he thought of the sky lamp, of the patchwork quilt his mother had made. "Well, hardly anybody. This is really something else."

"Today's technology is something else, as you put it." Dr. McEvoy toyed with the stapler on the desk. "It made the watch possible. And yet, ingenious as it is, the watch can be improved upon. In time"— she smiled at the pun—"I hope a watch something like this one will perform additional functions for you."

What else could he want to know? Dilly couldn't imagine. "Like what?"

She started clearing off the desktop, getting ready to work. "Oh, I would hope the watch could eventually include a device to indicate the varying magnitude of magnetic output. And possibly something could be added to measure the secondary electrical activity that accompanies magnetic action."

She directed one of her piercing looks at Dilly. "You are aware, aren't you, that where there is magnetism, there is electrical activity?"

"Sure." Dilly knew that in a vague sort of way. "Only I haven't thought about it. I just thought about the magnetism."

"And that's understandable. Dilloway—"

Dilly became alert. Her voice had taken on the tone he had come to recognize as a sign of something important about to be said.

"I believe we're ready to begin testing your magnetic muscle."

Wow! This was what he had been waiting for. And yet, the back of his neck prickled. He hadn't forgotten Dr. Mac's warning, spoken so long ago. "We don't know what might happen . . . happen . . . happen." The word echoed in his mind.

"We'll move upward to full release one step at a time, observing the effects on you with each increase. I want you to be aware of the electrical as well as the magnetic effects. Not just on yourself, but on your surroundings."

Electrical effects. Now there was something new to think about. Dilly's forehead puckered in concentration. "I guess," he said slowly, "if the electricity fed into something like a TV, it could knock it out."

"That would be aw-ful!" Dr. McEvoy drawled the word. "To knock out TV!"

Dilly had to laugh, the way she said it.

She returned to seriousness. "A gigantic surge could play havoc with an area's power source. Imagine. Lights would go off."

Dilly picked up on the idea. "So would refrigerators."

"It's all supposition, of course," said Dr. McEvoy. "But you get the idea. So we must consider the possible electrical consequences as well as the magnetic."

Dilly nodded gravely. There was a lot to think about.

Dr. McEvoy continued, her voice softer than the one she used when she was teaching him something. "Dilloway, this is one of those difficult decisions you alone can make. I want you to think hard about this for a few days. You can say yes or no."

"But I want to find out!" Dilly couldn't imagine stopping now, after all these weeks of training. "I've got to know."

"Good enough," Dr. McEvoy said briskly. "But mull it over anyway. And we don't have to start until you feel absolutely comfortable about moving ahead." She offered her hand. "All right?"

Dilly took it. "All right."

They shook on the agreement.

"Now, tell me. What have you been up to lately?" she asked.

Dilly grinned. "Want to see something? Want to see what I can do with—" He looked around the office and spotted a metal canister on the windowsill. "With the lid from that Gunpowder Tea box?"

"I'll bet I'm going to be surprised," said Dr. McEvoy.

Dilly removed the lid from the canister, wiping it free of dust from the chalk it now contained, testing it as he came back to the desk. Yes, there was enough iron in the lid to permit him to work with it. It was light enough, too.

"Watch me." He directed a pulse into his fingers, stroking the lid as he did so. "I'm magnetizing it," he explained, his eyes fixed on the circle of metal.

"Right." Dr. McEvoy was watching him closely.

"Okay," said Dilly. "Now." He balanced the lid on the tips of the fingers of his right hand. He let it rest there, then loosed a magnetic pulse. The metal lid rose above his fingers, seemingly cushioned on air. It remained that way for a long moment, then flipped over and clung to his fingers.

Dr. McEvoy was silent.

Dilly laughed. "Neat, huh?"

She let out a long breath. " 'Like poles repel each

other.' You've learned to use that principle. All on your own."

"I got kind of bored with paper clips," said Dilly.

Dr. McEvoy's eyes sparkled. "You are a wonderfully apt pupil. We'll do more with the magnetic repulsion thing, now that you've started working with it." She reached out and ruffled his hair. "Ah, but I'm proud of you, Dilloway."

Dilly glowed with pleasure.

A distant squeaking of wheels came from the corridor. The sound grew louder as something rolled nearer the office. Buckets clanked. Men called to each other.

"The janitors are here," said Dilly. "I've got to get on home. Contrary needs a run before dinner." He slipped on his backpack.

Dr. McEvoy rose with him and shrugged into her coat.

Dilly led the way into the hall. Dr. McEvoy closed the door behind them and they made their way down the corridor. Empty except for the cleaning crew, it had a faintly haunted air.

"Be careful, lady," called one of the men, swishing a mop around in great curving arcs. "Wet floors are slippery."

Dr. McEvoy thanked him. Stepping carefully around the shining, wet places, they made their way to the front entrance, and pushed through the unwieldy doors. Outside, the air was heavy with the threat of rain. Dr. McEvoy hurried to her car and Dilly, eager to get home to Contrary before the clouds opened up, ran to his bicycle.

Behind them, in the deserted school, the janitor who had spoken entered the office they had just left. He reached for the wastebasket, straightening as he started reading one of the discarded papers. As the metal container came up to desktop level, the canister lid slapped against it with a resounding clang.

Startled, he dropped the wastebasket. It clattered to the floor, spilling paper, the lid still clinging to it. Shaken, the man tried to separate the two objects. The lid held stubbornly. He could not break the magnetic tension.

Footsteps sounded in the corridor. "Holtz?" The voice was that of the crew foreman. "Get to one-eleven and give a hand to Kopeck."

Hastily the janitor gathered the scattered papers, flattened them, and stuffed them into his shirt. He placed the wastebasket in its customary spot beside the desk.

At the door, he looked back at it, shaking his head in puzzlement.

DILLY AND CONTRARY HAD RUN until Dilly was out of breath. Now he leaned against the rough bark of an oak tree, absent-mindedly watching Contrary explore the ragged borders of a vacant lot. His mind was back in Dr. McEvoy's office.

"Mull it over," she had said.

But he had already made up his mind. He wasn't going to put the brakes on now. He was going ahead with the big stuff, no matter what that might mean. The thing he had to think about was what might happen when he went to the max. Might it really hurt him? He had to be ready for that. He shivered.

Contrary came back to him, paused momentarily, and then set out for home at a purposeful trot, carefully avoiding the puddles on the sidewalk.

Dilly matched his pace. "You know, Con," he said, thinking, "I don't know where this is gonna end. It's one big adventure."

The thing about adventures—the words rose in his mind—*is they're full of surprises.*

"So even if I'm kind of spooked about it," Dilly said aloud, "I guess I'll go for the surprises."

Contrary took off at a full run. *Surprise me,* he seemed to be saying. *Beat me home. Dinner's waiting.*

Dilly ran to catch up with him.

Late the next day
well inside the entrance to a worked-out mine . . .

operatives Blunt, O'Mallet, and von Pfist huddled within the circle of light cast by Master Operative Gorey's flashlight. Blunt was finishing his report.

"My contact couldn't interpret his findings. He simply passed along the information and expressed bewilderment."

"The effect was most probably magnetic," the master operative said thoughtfully. "But how? How?"

"Sir." It was von Pfist. "Yesterday afternoon the boy was heard to express fear about some enterprise. 'Spooked' was the word he used."

"Then plans of some sort are afoot." Gorey spoke forcefully. "Something unusual is going on in that office. The boy may mean more to us than mere money. We'll take him. Now."

"The woman as well?" asked Blunt.

"The boy first." The master operative paced before them. "Later, the woman."

"The proposed camping trip would be a natural opportunity to pick him up," O'Mallet suggested.

"But you say the date for the trip is uncertain."

"My source is effective." O'Mallet's voice was tense. "I believe he can give us a date soon."

"We cannot wait." The master operative was firm. "We will set the time. Operative McHammer will take the boy to—"

"Sir? Sir," von Pfist pleaded, "to entrust this operation to an amateur like McHammer is—"

"No more!" Master Operative Gorey cut her off. "You say you are a professional. Follow orders like one!"

Operative von Pfist seemed to grow smaller within her trench coat. She did not speak again.

"Nothing can possibly go wrong," continued the master operative. "McHammer's role is simple. He has only to take the boy hiking. At an agreed-upon spot, we will move in. Now, synchronize your watches, if you please."

Arms were lifted.

"Five forty-two, thirty."

Watches were adjusted in the harsh glare of the master operative's flashlight.

"*Blunt: one forty-one. Von Pfist: one forty-seven. O'Mallet: one fifty-three. You will call Contacts at those times tomorrow for your assignments.*"

"*Sir!*" *murmured three hushed voices.*

The master operative pushed past them, leading the way up the packed earth of the tunnel. The operatives scrambled to stay within the circle of light. Near the entrance, he switched it off. Ahead, the opening to the mine was a gray square in the darkness.

Suddenly the air stirred. A flapping, a dry shuffling of wings, echoed behind them. Louder. Louder.

As one, the operatives dropped to the earth and covered their heads.

Small flitting forms poured from the depths of the mine and out into the darkening sky as thousands of bats emerged for the nightly hunt.

JEPSON WHIRTBY ARRIVED SATURDAY while
Dilly was still eating lunch. He came into the dining
room, togged out in the latest jogging clothes. They
looked brand new. His shoes were blindingly white.

"I'll just have coffee, my man," he said to Blackpool as he settled into a chair at the table. "Well,
old chap." He smiled broadly at Dilly. "Today's the
day."

"It's been raining all week," protested Dilly.
"Hiking won't be any fun. The fields and woods will
be wet."

"Ah, but the day is beautiful. Look at the sunshine
out there." Whirtby nodded toward the window. "I
knew it would be. I've kept in touch with the weather
service this week."

Mrs. Blackpool bustled in with coffee. Whirtby
spooned sugar into it and with great care filled it
nearly to the rim with cream.

Glumly, Dilly dug into his apple tart. The terrible thing about being a kid was that sometimes you had to do what grown-ups told you to do, even grown-ups like Squirtby.

He didn't want to go hiking with Squirtby. But he hadn't figured a way to avoid it. And Squirtby, he knew, didn't want to go hiking with him. Squirtby only wanted to make points with Mr. Orbed.

Dilly didn't like the way Squirtby did things just to impress Mr. Orbed. He didn't like being called "old chap." He didn't like the way Squirtby called Blackpool "my man." He didn't, he realized at that moment, like anything about Jepson Whirtby. The thought surprised him. He hadn't disliked many people in his life.

"Well, perhaps we can't go into the fields," said Whirtby. "But there must be many pleasant byways we can explore. Why, I've always wanted to see Lumber Baron Lookout."

Movement outside the window drew Dilly's eyes away from the apple tart. Jessica rolled to a stop on her bicycle. Matt and Bryan followed her, guiding an empty bicycle between them. Jessica made broad gestures toward the front of the house, and then the three of them disappeared around the corner.

"Excuse me." Dilly leaped up. "I'll be right back." He ran for the front door.

"Is that him sitting there at the table?" hissed Matt.

"You said you didn't want to go hiking with him," Jessica said softly. "If you've got to go, we'll go with you."

"We can go on a bike hike," Bryan whispered. "We brought my dad's bike for him to ride."

A grin spread across Dilly's face. Friends! Friends made up for terrible grown-ups! "Come on," he whispered. Then he raised his voice for Jepson Whirtby's ears. "I'd like you all to meet Mr. Whirtby."

They followed him to the dining room.

"Mr. Whirtby," Dilly said formally, "these are my friends Jessica and Matt and Bryan. They're coming with us."

"Oh, but—" Whirtby looked alarmed. "But I don't think—I mean, you and I could have a nice walk by ourselves."

"We're going on a bike hike," said Dilly.

Jepson Whirtby turned white. "I haven't ridden a bicycle since I was a child. I'm sure I can't ride one."

Matt laughed. "Nobody forgets how to ride a bike! It's like swimming. Once you've learned, you can't not know how."

Jessica turned on her most angelic smile. "I gave up a babysitting job just so I could come with you today."

"I passed on a good-paying leaf-raking job," said Bryan.

"Let's go!" whooped Dilly before Whirtby could think of something to prevent Bryan and Matt and Jessica from joining them. He headed for the front door. The others tumbled after him. Contrary shot out of the library and joined them with a belling "ah-oooo!"

A pale Jepson Whirtby followed, wringing his hands. "Well, if you insist. But must that dog accompany us?"

"Where I go, Contrary goes," Dilly said firmly. "He likes to run in the country."

They all mounted their bikes. One bicycle remained standing. Whirtby approached it warily. He reached down awkwardly and raised the kick stand with his hand, then settled onto the saddle.

Matt rolled down the drive and onto Josephine Street. The others spun after him.

Dilly looked over his shoulder. Whirtby was wobbling dangerously, the front wheel of his bicycle turning from left to right as he tried to stay upright.

Bryan turned back. He rode in circles around Whirtby. "Don't try to ride slow," he called. "Pedal faster. It's easier to go straight." Then he left Whirtby to his own efforts. "He'll get better as he rides," he told the others cheerfully.

They rode slower than they normally did, but

Whirtby remained a half block behind them, sitting rigidly upright, pedaling sedately. He caught up with them at last as they waited to cross an intersection.

"Oh, say now," he called brightly. "Why don't we all head out toward Lumber Baron Lookout? I hear the view is beautiful."

"But that's way up on top of Hennessy Hill," said Jessica. "Hennessy Hill's the tallest hill around here."

"You've got to practice before you tackle that," Bryan said kindly as he pushed off.

"Oh, but I—"

Nobody heard him. They were already crossing the intersection.

Looking at his watch, Whirtby got off to another wobbly start and followed them.

MEANWHILE, A VAN MADE ITS WAY out of a muddy road on the lower slopes of Hennessy Hill. Spinning its wheels, spraying mud, it turned onto Logging Truck Road and headed uphill, leaving a trail of muddy tracks on the blacktop.

FAR AHEAD OF WHIRTBY, on River Road, Dilly and the others left their bikes and went into a field to check out some cattails. They were heading back toward the road, through the tall, wet grass, when Whirtby spotted them. He dropped his bicycle at the roadside and started toward the field.

"Wait!" Dilly yelled. "It's mighty wet in here. You'll get soaked." His voice trailed away.

Whirtby had already waded into the grass. He stood, looking down at his feet. They were, Dilly knew, squishing in mud.

Whirtby gave a slightly sick smile as they neared him. "Were you checking out the local flora?"

"Flora?" muttered Matt. "Where's this guy coming from!"

Jessica explained sweetly that the rain had ruined the cattails. "There are lots of teasels, though. Maybe we can come back for them when they dry off. Mr. Kennedy asked me to find some interesting weeds for homeroom."

"Very interesting." Whirtby sounded not at all interested. "Tell me, how far are we from Lumber Baron Lookout?"

THE VAN WAS PARKED at the lookout. Operatives O'Mallet and Blunt lounged against the stone parapet, looking out over the hills.

"Why didn't von Pfist come with us?" asked Blunt.

O'Mallet shrugged. "I saw her this morning. She wasn't around at fourteen hundred, though. Contacts said to leave without her. Maybe they sent her out on another assignment."

"Odd," muttered Blunt. "I wouldn't have expected her to miss the pickup in this operation."

O'Mallet looked at his watch. "McHammer and the kid should be getting here soon."

DILLY, MATT, JESSICA, AND BRYAN were perched on a fence at the airport. A jittery Whirtby leaned on it next to them. They were watching a small plane take off and land, take off and land again. Someone was having a flying lesson.

"I heard there might be a glider here today," said Matt.

"We can wait around," said Dilly. "Maybe it'll come. We've got all afternoon."

Whirtby looked pained. "Well, not quite all afternoon. I must get back to town today." With great control he added casually, "And I really would like to see the view from the lookout."

Dilly turned to study him. "You know, you're really not ready for that. You haven't been on a bike since you were a kid. You're going to be mighty stiff tomorrow."

"Well, old chap"—Whirtby gave his best us-guys-together smile—"it might be worth it, for that spectacular view."

"Tell you what," said Bryan, "let's go to the fair

grounds. That's on the way. Then if you still want to go up there . . ."

They swung onto their bikes, and with Contrary racing in and out among them, headed down the road.

Groaning, Whirtby tried to sprint after them.

BLUNT LOOKED AT HIS WATCH. The golden afternoon sun lit up the western part of the sky. "Should've been here half an hour ago."

"Maybe von Pfist was onto something, about not trusting an amateur with a key move in an operation like this," said O'Mallet.

BUILDINGS AT THE FAIR GROUNDS were boarded up for the winter. But the posters and signs reminded everybody of the events of the summer.

"I hit the bull's eye three times in a row and the clown got dumped into the tank three times," chortled Jessica. "My throwing arm's in pretty good shape."

"My dad made the gong ring when he swung that sledgehammer," said Matt. "And two of our cows took blue ribbons."

Whirtby cut in. "Now, see here!"

They looked at him, startled.

"I'm the grown-up in this group." He drew himself up with as much dignity as his wet jogging suit and muddy shoes permitted. "And I say we are going to Lumber Baron Lookout. We are g-g-going," he stuttered, "n-n-now!"

Dilly and the others exchanged looks and shrugged. What had caused this outburst?

"You really want to go up there?" Dilly said good-naturedly. "Okay. I'll go with you." Squirtby was, after all, his problem. No need to make the others go on a hard ride like that.

"We'll come with you," said Jessica.

"Oh, there's no need to put yourself out," Whirtby said hastily. "Dilloway and I will be just fine."

"Aw, we'll come," said Bryan.

"Sure, why not?" said Matt.

OPERATIVE BLUNT'S JAW WAS SET. "I say we wait another half hour. If they don't turn up, we leave. It'll be dark soon."

LOOKING BACK, Dilly saw that Whirtby was following without too much difficulty. He looked happier, now that they were on their way up to the lookout. Dilly wondered, though, how he'd manage higher up on the hillside where Logging Truck Road was steeper.

Ahead, Contrary stopped at the turnoff onto the undeveloped road that led to the fenced compound. He lifted a muddy forepaw in disgust.

Bryan moved up beside Dilly, his eyes on the trail of dried mud that led out onto the road ahead of them. "Whoever was driving that car was lucky he didn't get stuck there."

The road upward became steeper. Dilly stood up to pedal. The others followed his lead. Whirtby, wobbling again, was beginning to puff. He fell behind.

Faintly, from above, came the sound of a car approaching, its tires squealing on the curves.

Dilly recognized the place where he and Contrary ate lunch the day before school began. Contrary recognized it, too. He dashed off to explore.

"Maybe we'd better pull over until that car passes," called Dilly.

The screeching of tires was louder now. The car sounded as though it was in second gear, but it was still coming on fast.

As they watched, a van careened around the curve ahead. It passed them at high speed, then screeched to a halt. A man leaned out and looked back at them. Suddenly the van went into reverse, backed up, and jerked to a stop.

Two men leaped out. One pulled open the doors at the back. Moving fast, they pushed aside Matt, Jessica, Bryan.

"Watch it!" Matt hollered, going at them with his fists.

"What do you think you're doing?" yelled Bryan, grabbing at one of the men.

The burliest of the men got hold of Dilly and pulled him, kicking and fighting, toward the van.

"Let me go!" Dilly struggled with the muscular arms that held him. "Con—" A hand clapped over his open mouth. He bit down hard.

"Ai!" The man pulled his hand away.

Jessica fastened herself to his arm. "You let Dilly go!" The man shook her off as he might have a kitten. She landed in a clump of bushes, stunned.

"Contrary!" Dilly shouted again. "Con—" A white cloth clapped over his mouth, stifling the call. What was that awful smell? Fighting, breathing hard, he felt as though his head was spinning.

The man thrust him into the van and jumped in after him, slamming the door. The other man punched and shoved Matt and Bryan, sending them flying. Then he leaped into the driver's seat.

"What's going on?" shouted Whirtby, approaching from down the road. He dropped his bike and ran toward the moving van, pulled open a door, and flung himself inside.

The van moved away on squealing tires.

Contrary, emerging from the woods, bounded after it, a blur of flying feet and flapping ears.

WHERE WAS HE? Dilly's head hurt. He tasted—no, he smelled—something funny, something sickeningly sweet. It made his stomach turn over. He swallowed and opened his eyes.

He was in a high-ceilinged room, lying on something soft. People were talking. They didn't notice him open his eyes. He closed them. He had to think. What was happening?

Bits of memory, like fragments of a torn picture, came back. Kick! Fight! Don't let that guy hold you. Bite! Ah. Got his thumb. Yelp! Thumb yanked away. Kick! Right into somebody's stomach. Ooof! Something about a car, a van. Something about being pushed into the van. Something white coming at him, covering his face. The sweetish smell. Nothing more.

His head whirled. What was that sound? Like water splashing. He opened his eyes. Just a slit.

Was that a fountain over there? The lights and the people swirled together. He closed his eyes.

Think. Think. Somebody had grabbed him. Why? What were they going to do to him? Were the other kids here, too?

Again, a slight lifting of his eyelids. Again the dizzying whirl of lights and people. Grown people. No kids. No Matt or Bryan or Jessica. Good.

"IF IT HADN'T BEEN . . ." The words roared, then sank to a murmur. ". . . for those pesky friends of his . . . I WOULD'VE GOT HIM . . . there on time." The voice was on a string swinging over him, near, far, loud, soft. "OH, I SAY . . ."

That voice! Squirtby was here—wherever "here" was.

Had to think. Keep his wits. What did he have going for him? They didn't know he was awake. That was good. He had his magnetism. Maybe that was good. But how to use it?

From somewhere deep in his mind a thought floated upward. Don't talk. Listen. Get as much information as you can. Yes. That's what he would do. Listen.

Another voice. "HE SHOULD BE COMING AROUND." Loud. Then soft. "How much of that stuff did you let him inhale?"

His head throbbed. The sickeningly sweet smell

wouldn't go away. He swallowed, swallowed again. His stomach lurched.

Slap-slap. Someone slapping his face lightly.

"OH, I SAY, OLD CHAP. Wake up now. IT'S TIME to open YOUR EYES."

Dilly opened his eyes. And his mouth. He threw up all over Jepson Whirtby.

Several men stood around him. One of them wiped his face with a damp cloth. "BREATHE DEEP, breathe deep."

He breathed deep.

"He's coming around." He remembered that voice. The arm around his shoulders helping him sit up felt vaguely familiar. "Feeling better?"

He shoved the arm away. "Where am I?" he whispered weakly.

"You're quite safe," said the man with the cool cloth, offering him a glass of water. "Nobody is going to hurt you."

Dilly took the glass, noticing with satisfaction that the hand holding it had a bandage on the thumb. He sniffed the water. It smelled okay. He sipped it. No taste except a good icy-water taste. Nothing in it. He sipped again, feeling better, looking around.

Whirtby had disappeared. A small man paced back and forth before the couch where Dilly sat. He moved nervously with short, jerky steps. He was dressed in black, except for his jogging shoes. A halo of wild hair stood out around his head. He turned round, bulging eyes on Dilly.

"Why am I here?" Dilly demanded. "What do you want with me? And who in heck are you?"

The man waved the others away with a flip of his hand. They departed silently. His lips, pursed, webbed around with tiny wrinkles, parted in a smile. "Think of me as your friend," he said softly.

Sure I will, thought Dilly. And you can think of me as Santa Claus.

"I am," said the man, "Dr. Keenwit. You will be detained here for a short time. We expect to hear from your guardians at the bank soon. Then you will be released."

The man's meaning became clear. "You mean I'm kidnapped? You're holding me for ransom?" Dilly's eyes were wide.

"Ah, but nothing so crude." The bulging eyes rolled upward in distaste. "You are, shall we say, security on a loan."

"But you're not about to let me just pick up and leave," Dilly said flatly, looking around.

A large window in the far wall opened onto what looked like a computer room. People were at work among the equipment. No door opened into the area. But there was one off to the right of the window. Where did that lead? Maybe beyond it was another door leading to the outside.

The man saw his searching glance. "Even if you found our exit door, you wouldn't be able to open it. Just let me add this thought—perhaps, when you understand our cause, you will not want to leave."

Dilly stared at the man.

The bulging eyes glinted. "When you learn about our operation, your choice may be to remain with us, to use your special abilities to help the world."

Special abilities? Dilly was instantly alert. What did this guy know? He's bluffing, said his inner voice, trying to get you to tell something.

"Dr. McEvoy's reputation for brilliance goes before her." Dr. Keenwit's pacing speeded up, became a queer little bouncing step. He clasped and unclasped his hands. "She would not devote time to a pupil who had nothing special to offer."

"Hey!" Dilly put on a look of innocence. "She's helping all of us kids with our projects for the science fair. She just likes kids."

"But you"—the man stopped abruptly before him, leaned close, spoke in a whisper—"more than any other. You have visited her home."

Dilly didn't let his surprise show. But, but, how did this guy know that?

"Your meetings with her are more frequent than

other students'. They last longer. Perhaps you would like to tell me about them, about your work with . . . magnetism?"

Somebody had been watching him for sure! It wasn't Blackpool. Who, then? Dilly licked his lips. He had to find out more.

"What did you mean, your 'cause'?" he demanded.

Dr. Keenwit clasped his hands behind him, looking down at Dilly. "I am brilliant," he said quietly. "It is said in some quarters that I am the reigning genius of the world." He made the statement in tones so ordinary that he might have been commenting on the weather.

Dilly rubbed his forehead. This situation was getting more weird by the minute. What kind of guy went around bragging that he was the smartest man in the world?

"And I—" The bulging amber eyes blinked rapidly. "I have a plan for the world that is so good" —he crooned the word—"so great, that everyone will be happy. As everyone is meant to be."

A shiver ran up Dilly's spine. This guy was . . . He couldn't find a word for it. He spoke carefully. "Your, uh, plan for the world. Did you make it up all by yourself?"

Dr. Keenwit looked past Dilly, into the perfect future he envisioned. "In the beginning, the plan was mine alone. But as I created the Great Harmonizer, my vision grew. It is the Great Harmonizer that will create the patterns of the future. Come. I will show you."

Dilly stood. What in heck was a harmonizer? Well, as long as he was a prisoner, he might as well find out as much as he could about this place.

As they crossed the great hall, moving among the groups of comfortable furniture, Dilly took in the fountain with its play of tossing waters, a computer terminal set near one wall, an empty picture frame above it. He had only a minute to wonder about the oddness of an empty picture frame before Dr. Keenwit led him through the door. They stood in a windowed corridor. Dilly was aware of the cool wash of humidity-controlled air.

The man gestured to a room on the right. Rows of shelves filled it. They were jammed with stacks of envelopes, reels of tape, boxes spilling over with papers. "Information," he said, "gathered from all points of the compass. The latest technology. Scientific information. Data from large corporations, universities, research laboratories. Even from governments. It's raw as it's brought in, of course. It will be processed into compatible form for use in the Great Harmonizer."

"You mean they share information with you?" If

everybody was willing to give information to this guy, maybe . . .

"Share!" Dr. Keenwit snorted. "My boy, the first rule of life seems to be to share nothing. No. I buy information. In every company, every government, every laboratory, there are people who understand the value of the information that surrounds them."

Dilly took that in. "You mean," he said slowly, "that people steal information and you pay them for it."

"Ooo-oo-ah!" Dr. Keenwit laughed. "You do see things in a black-and-white manner. I prefer to think these people are willing to, shall we say, take part in a new vision."

He had been moving as they talked. He paused now before the room Dilly had glimpsed from the great hall. "You see there"—he moved on—"the raw information being changed into my uniform system."

He led the way into a cabinet-lined room. "The most unusual library in the world," he said. "My disk library." He looked around, rubbing his hands, gloating.

Dilly watched him, fascinated. The man looked like a miser counting his gold. Dilly had never seen a miser. But he was sure this was what one looked like.

Dr. Keenwit let out a low chuckle. "Mine," he

muttered, "all mine." He turned glittering eyes on Dilly. "The information stored here is what makes the world run. Oh, what others would give for what I have here!"

Dilly felt chilled. He was kidnapped. He should feel scared for himself. And he was. But suddenly he was even more afraid for— But who was he scared for? "Do lots of people know about you?" He didn't know what to call all of this. "And your work?" he finished.

The unblinking, bulging eyes fixed on him. "Our work is for the present a hidden treasure. But soon, soon, we shall share it with the world." Dr. Keenwit moved out of the room, into the corridor.

Dilly followed him. But now I know about it, he thought. Is he going to let me go, knowing about it, when the bank gives him whatever he's asked for?

Dr. Keenwit stopped before another door. "Here!" His voice was hushed, reverent. He flung open the door. "And here is the Great Harmonizer. The synchronizer. The weaver of wonders and of the future happiness of people everywhere."

Dilly felt as though he was being presented to an ancient emperor, as though he was expected to kneel and touch his forehead to the floor. But this was no emperor.

At the center of the shadowed room, lit by spotlights, was a box, tall as a man, a faintly glistening blue. Extensions on either side reached forward, like arms. An ornate figure 8 in silver, glinting under the lights, embellished the surface facing the door.

Dilly had expected more from something called the Great Harmonizer. But this! "Why, it's just a computer," he said, "a big computer."

"Ah, boy, have you no vision?" Dr. Keenwit's voice rose. His words tumbled breathlessly one over the other. "Disks from my library go in. Out come beautiful plans. Pictures of the future. The end result of any action anywhere will be shown. If it's good, the action will be allowed to proceed. If the result would be unfortunate, the action will be stopped. At once."

In his clear-minded way, Dilly went straight to the heart of things. "So this bunch of circuit boards is going to lay down the rules for everybody."

Dr. Keenwit looked pained. "But of course you must know that behind every computer is a mind."

"Yours," Dilly said relentlessly. "So you're going to tell everybody in the world what to do."

"Well, I, as its creator, will make certain judgments." Dr. Keenwit made a poor attempt to look modest. "Yes, the Great Harmonizer and I will do that."

Dilly wanted to say, "I think you're a first-class nut." He wanted to say, "Not only that, you're dangerous." But he kept his head. He had to figure a way to get out of here. He was a prisoner. It was best not to insult this guy.

"I can see that you are not yet convinced of the worthiness of the cause," said Dr. Keenwit. "For a young boy, you are remarkably rigid. You should be open to new ideas, to new ways of doing things. Come. Let me show you something else."

Dilly followed him back the way they had come. He looked at his watch. He'd been here for a long time. Dinnertime had come and gone. Not that he cared, with the state of his stomach earlier. But he was tired. Was he going to be allowed to get some sleep?

Back in the great hall, Dr. Keenwit went to the computer terminal. He pressed a key. The fountain in the center of the room lit from within. The jets changed and shifted colors. "A small amusement," he said, seating himself at the keyboard. He touched the keys. The monitor screen glowed. "Now watch," he said.

Colors flowed onto the screen, moving, shading, forming, fading, giving place to other colors.

"No two patterns will ever be alike," he said over his shoulder. "The Great Harmonizer is at work. Look up, if you please." He motioned to the picture frame above the screen.

It was no longer empty. The design on the screen

was coming to life in the frame, a composition of luminous colors that deepened as Dilly watched.

"I will now make the picture semipermanent," said Dr. Keenwit, doing something with the keys. "No mere artist could do anything so glorious."

Fascinated in spite of himself, Dilly stared. The colors were beautiful. But the picture didn't grab his attention and make him feel good. If anything, it made him feel numb.

"And listen." Dr. Keenwit was now flicking keys wildly. Music filled the room. "Composed by no mere human!" He chortled delightedly.

The tones were clear, pure, electronic. They mingled, became chords, flowed into melody. And yet, somehow, the music didn't make Dilly's feet want to dance.

Dr. Keenwit removed his hands from the keys. The music continued. He lifted his voice to be heard. "Without the need to work at painting or writing music or poetry—oh, yes, the Great Harmonizer will one day write poetry—people will be able to simply sit back and enjoy these things. And I, I, Dr. Keenwit, give this to the world. My creation, the Great Harmonizer, and I—"

Noise, suddenly, came from somewhere, cutting through the music. Grating, thumping sounds, growing louder, louder.

Dr. Keenwit leaped to his feet. He was pale. "What?" he shouted. "What is that?"

Confused, Dilly looked around. His eyes followed Dr. Keenwit's to the wall off to the right. Was that wall moving? Was it bending inward?

He stood among the flashing lights of the fountain, amid the rising sound of the music, as a horn began to blare. A voice rose above the grating, the thumping, the crashing, above the horn—a mechanical voice.

"Intruder . . . *intruder* . . . INTRUDER . . ."

LIGHTS FLARED. Men began to pour out of the inner rooms.

The warning system continued its raucous bleat.

"INTRUD—" The mechanical voice changed its message. "TO YOUR STATIONS. TO YOUR STATIONS. TO YOUR STATIONS."

The grating, grinding, thumping noises swelled, coming closer.

Dilly shrank back toward the shimmering spill of the fountain, staring at the wall that seemed to be the source of the noise. THUD. What in heck was going on?

A jagged line snaked up the wall. It widened and became a crack. THUD. An opening appeared in the crack. THUD. Something on the other side of the wall battered it and the opening became a hole. Dirt and cinderblocks pushed into the room. Light reflected off metal on the other side of the hole, off something shiny and curved. It was the blade of an earth mover.

Relief washed over Dilly. Somebody was coming to get him. And with the relief, delight bubbled upward. That was a bulldozer breaking down the wall! It had to be Jessica's bulldozer! And nobody could be at the controls but Matt.

With a powerful thrust, the bulldozer opened the hole completely. Dirt, grass, roots, cinderblocks, two-by-fours tumbled into the room. Dust billowed upward in clouds, dimming the lights.

A small form hurtled through the opening, through the clouds of dust, and raced to Dilly. Contrary rolled over and over around his feet, wriggling in delight.

Dilly dropped to his knees and gathered him up. "Con, old boy, I've never been so glad to see you. I'm happier to see you than you are to see me!"

Contrary kissed him with a great, wet swipe of his tongue. Dilly laughed. "Did you bring people here, boy? Is that how the kids found me? I wish you could tell me where I am, anyway." He squinted into the dust, into pandemonium.

The noise was deafening. The music still played. The horn still blared. The mechanical voice changed its message again. "FIGHT. FIGHT. FIGHT."

And people were fighting.

Dr. Keenwit had leaped up onto a table and was yelling orders.

Matt and Bryan and Jessica were nowhere in sight. But there was Blackpool. As Dilly watched, he picked up a man, held him overhead, and slammed him to the floor.

There! Over there! Was that Mr. Orbed? Dilly watched in wonder. Was Mr. Orbed fencing with his gold-headed walking stick?

Light on his toes, the round little man danced forward, forward, thrusting, then backward, parrying, as his adversary tried to get past the walking stick. Light glinted on the walking stick. No walking stick, that! It was a sword! Forward again, forward, thrusting. Forward. Thrust. The other man met the sword and with a look of astonishment went down.

"EEE-YIII!" Dilly turned. His mouth fell open as Mrs. Blackpool delivered a karate chop. The man folded like an old coat crumpling to the floor.

Gentle, timid Mrs. Blackpool? Karate?

With an intake of breath, Dilly saw a man approaching her from behind. At the same instant, Contrary saw, too. With a yelp he leaped from Dilly's arms, cut through the melee, and fastened his teeth in the man's leg.

The man's mouth opened in a howl. He gave a powerful shake of his leg. Contrary went flying. Mrs.

Blackpool turned. Her face reddened with anger. You . . . hurt . . . Contrary. Dilly saw her mouth form the words.

"Kiiii-YAH!" She dropped the man with a kick.

Beyond her, Blackpool had hold of someone around the middle, squeezing, squeezing. The man's face turned purple. He went limp. Blackpool flung him against a wall. Bodies lay around Blackpool.

Dilly's every instinct was to leap into the middle of things. He did, after all, know a little judo. But not enough, he decided, to make a difference in this battle. He had only one advantage and this wasn't where it could be put to its best use. There was something that had to be done.

He inched away from the fountain, his eyes on Dr. Keenwit, on the battle scene, moving backward. Nobody must see him leave.

He reached the corridor, pushed through the door, and ran. Past the room that held all the "raw" information from informants. Past the computer room where that information was transferred onto disks.

He slid to a stop at the entrance to the disk library, looking over his shoulder to see whether he had been followed. The corridor was empty. He stepped into the room and leaned against the wall, breathing deeply, looking around. He had to be sure of what he was about to do.

"The most unusual library in the world," Dr. Keenwit had called it. Dilly could only guess at the kind of information contained here in microscopic magnetic patterns on the thousands of disks. Sensitive information. Stolen information. The closely guarded secrets of governments, scientists, thinkers of every kind. And all of it was to be used to further Dr. Keenwit's twisted need for power.

Darting through the room, he slid open the doors of the cabinets. Then he began moving deliberately among them, reaching into them, relaxing, feeling the familiar tingling in his fingers.

He ran his hands over the disks almost lovingly, stroking them, creating magnetic fields around them, erasing the minute magnetic patterns on the coated surfaces, wiping out the coded information.

Vibrations from his wristwatch sensor traveled up his arm. Looking down, he saw that his arm quivered, that his hands were turning red. He felt curiously separated from that arm, from those hands. He knew only that he was releasing more magnetism than ever before.

In a far corner of his mind he was faintly aware of distant bedlam. He shut it out. His thoughts concentrated on this room, these flat, round objects, and the magnetic power that streamed from his fingers.

Finished at last, he put out a hand to steady himself. The room tilted. He shook his head to clear it, looking around.

Anyone entering the disk library might wonder about the open doors of the cabinets. But there was no other sign of the chaos he had created. Only when the disks were entered into a computer would someone find that they had become pieces of—nothing. He had wiped out Dr. Keenwit's work. There was only one more thing that remained to be done.

He felt groggy and weak. Staggering slightly, he made his way to the room that held the Great Harmonizer.

He stared at the harmless-looking blue box, at the decorative figure 8. Place a finger on the eight, trace it, and there was no natural stopping place, no exit. A finger could just keep moving on, on, forever, on an endless, repeated track.

Dr. Keenwit's boasting aside, the Great Harmonizer was in fact a marvel of human invention.

It could, he had no doubt of it, analyze actions and anticipate their future outcome.

It could, he was certain, "harmonize" widely varied information into patterns that had never been thought of by the human mind, that would be totally new, that could direct the future.

The Great Harmonizer did, in fact, create remarkable music, dazzling artwork. He had witnessed that as Dr. Keenwit's proof of what his invention could do. But the music chilled the heart. The artwork numbed the spirit. And so might the Great Harmonizer's plans chill, numb, the people it would control.

In the hands of even the most trustworthy person, the Great Harmonizer was awe inspiring. In the hands of a Dr. Keenwit, it was a thing to inspire dread.

Dilly knew what he must do. The decision had to be his alone. There was nobody here to talk to. If only Dr. Mac . . .

Her words came back to him. "We don't know what might happen when you release magnetism in its full strength. I don't want you to be hurt."

Uneasiness tugged at him. He shrugged it aside. I don't want to be hurt, either, he thought. But he couldn't wait to test his output one small step at a time. The Great Harmonizer was here, now.

He moved around it to the back where panels could be removed. Inside were the circuit boards that were the heart of the thing. He thrust his hands in among them, curling his fingers around the wires.

"What are you doing? Wretched boy, get away from there!"

Dilly looked over his shoulder.

Dr. Keenwit rushed at him. "I command you to

stop whatever it is you are doing." The words rose in a mad shriek. "Stop!"

The blazing, bulging eyes were the last thing Dilly saw as magnetism surged from his hands. His body quivered. Blackness swallowed him.

DARKNESS CLAIMED THE MANY ROOMS in the hillside, a smothering blackness. With it, all sound ceased. The warning horn droned to a deep tone and failed. The mechanical voice faded in midword. The music sighed into stillness. And the clangor of battle in the great hall stopped abruptly. No voice broke the silence.

Moments passed. Then a faint light made its presence known. The luminous glow of moonlight filled the massive hole punched through the wall.

There was a rustling, a stir in the great hall. A figure hobbled toward the opening, stood for an instant silhouetted against the night sky, then crept through and disappeared into the night. Others followed.

"Mrs. Blackpool?" Mr. Orbed spoke urgently. "Blackpool? Are you all right?"

"Of course!" The note of reproach in the soft voice

seemed to say that Mrs. Blackpool did not welcome the suggestion that she might not be all right.

"Drat! Can't see a blasted thing." That was Blackpool. "I keep stumbling over bodies."

Bryan, Jessica, and Matt darted in from outside, Dr. McEvoy close behind them. Disoriented by the blackness into which they plunged, they stopped in confusion, bumping into each other, all speaking at once. "Hey, what's going on in here?" "Is Dilly here?" "Is Dilloway all right?" "Dilll-yyy! It's us. Where are you?"

There was no answer.

"Hold it," Mr. Orbed called. "Wait there, if you please. We need light."

"I'll get the emergency floodlamp out of the car," said Blackpool.

His progress through the darkness was punctuated with the sounds of furniture bumped out of place, of something crashing to the floor, of muttered exclamations. At last he could be seen in the light of the opening. He went out into the moonlight. When he returned he trotted behind the brilliant beam of a floodlamp. Dr. McEvoy and Jessica, Matt, and Bryan crowded around him.

"We saw people come out of here," Bryan said excitedly. "Should we follow them?"

"Let them go." The light shone on Mr. Orbed.

His sword had become once more the harmless-looking walking stick. He looked searchingly into the shadows. "Dilloway? Lad? Where are you?"

Blackpool swept the great hall with his light. Crumpled figures on the floor stirred and groaned. The beam flashed on the window at the back of the room. Contrary stood on his hind legs, pawing at the door there.

"Through that door!" shouted Mr. Orbed, bounding toward it. "Quick!"

Blackpool got there first, thrusting it open. Contrary shot through and disappeared.

The others pushed into the corridor, close to Blackpool and the light that burrowed into the blackness. Their reflections glared harshly off the windows that lined the narrow space.

"Dilll-yyy!"

"Where are you?"

"Can you answer us?"

Their voices carried into the deserted rooms.

And still there was no reply.

"Make any kind of noise you can, lad," called Mr. Orbed. "Bang on the walls."

They held their breaths, listening. A far-away whine sounded in the silence.

"That's Contrary! He's found him!"

"Don't make so much noise. Listen for Con."

Moving quietly, then, they let Contrary direct

them. And so they discovered Dilly. He lay sprawled on the floor beside the Great Harmonizer. Contrary was licking his face.

Dr. McEvoy crossed the room in a bound, knelt, and scooped him up into her arms. She held a finger against the pulse point on his temple.

"Is he hurt bad?" Jessica's voice trembled.

"I'm not sure." Dr. McEvoy moved Dilly's face from side to side, looking for signs of injury. There were none. She picked up one of his hands, then the other. She made no comment on their unusual redness.

"Maybe we should make a run for the hospital," said Blackpool. "I'll carry him. I can do it without jarring him." He knelt beside Dr. McEvoy.

She stroked Dilly's cheek. "Dilloway," she said softly.

He stirred.

"I think he's coming around," she said, and again, louder, "Dilloway?"

"It's time to wake up and say hello to your friends, lad," said Mr. Orbed. He too crouched beside Dilly.

Dilly's eyelids fluttered. He felt strong warm arms holding him. He felt Contrary's furry wriggling body. He opened his eyes and looked up at Dr. McEvoy. "Hi, Dr. Mac." He took a deep, shuddering breath. "See? I'm okay. I can do it. I'm okay."

There was a sigh of relief from Jessica. "He's okay!"

"What's he mean?" asked Matt. "What can he do?"

There was understanding in Dr. McEvoy's eyes as she looked down at Dilly. She smiled. "So. You found out," she said softly. She raised her voice, still looking down at him. "I think, Matthew," she said, "that Dilloway means he can take care of himself."

"Nobody ever thought he couldn't!" said Bryan.

Dilly sat up, blinking in the glare of the floodlamp, looking around. "The lights went out," he said matter of factly, and, "I wonder what happened to Dr. Keenwit."

"Something"—Mr. Orbed sent a piercing look at Dilly—"knocked out the electrical system. As for anybody else, we seem to be here alone now."

Dilly pushed himself to his feet. He was woozy. But he was excited and proud as well. If the electrical system was out, it was because he had sent a sudden burst of power into it. That meant the Great Harmonizer was damaged. Maybe it was beyond repair. He had done a good thing. He knew he had.

And he wasn't kidnapped anymore, either. His friends, all of them, were here. He was safe.

"Can we go home now?" he asked.

THE BULLDOZER STOOD near the tumbled earth around the opening. Some distance away was its transport trailer. Dilly took that in as they emerged at a run from the underground chambers.

"You drove the trailer!" he said to Matt, awed.

"Had to," said Matt. "It was the only way to get the bulldozer here."

"Did you ever drive one before?" Dilly asked, looking back, as Blackpool herded them toward the car.

"Nope. But the guy who delivers feed to the farm let me see the stuff in the cab of his semi once. I drove real slow."

"No more palaver," Blackpool barked. "I want us out of here."

"Blackpool's right," Mr. Orbed called. "We have no assurance things won't erupt again."

"But how did you know where I was?" Dilly whispered as everyone crowded into the car.

"Remember the mud on the road?" Bryan whispered back. "We followed it after those guys grabbed you. The van turned back into the mud and left a trail right up to the fence."

Blackpool slammed doors and leaped into the driver's seat. They moved out onto the dirt road, drove the short distance to Logging Truck Road, and headed toward town. Behind them, figures continued to creep out of the battered entrance on the hillside.

"Jess," said Bryan, "what are you going to tell

your dad? I mean, about taking the keys and every-thing?"

"Don't know," she admitted uneasily. "He keeps telling me it's my bulldozer." She hunched her shoulders and huddled into the corner of the seat. "But now we've left it way out here in the country, and . . . and . . ."

"There's a lot to sort out," said Dr. McEvoy. Her eyes met Mr. Orbed's. "Maybe everyone should spend the night at the house?"

"Excellent idea!" He thumped the gold-headed walking stick on the floor. "We can all have some-thing to eat and talk about what happened."

Matt and Bryan and Jessica liked that idea. Es-pecially Jessica.

"I'll call your parents, then," said Dr. McEvoy.

Mr. Orbed turned to Jessica. "And I'll call your father, my dear, and make arrangements to see him early tomorrow morning about the bulldozer." He removed his glasses and rubbed his eyes. "But what," he murmured distractedly to himself, "what pre-cisely am I going to tell the man!"

As they neared the lights of Hennessy Depot, Mrs. Blackpool started reviewing the contents of the refrigerator. "There's some of that roast beef for sandwiches," she said thoughtfully. "And the baked beans from yesterday."

Dilly squirmed forward through the crush of bodies. Matt and Bryan were comparing notes on how long it had taken them to get the bulldozer to the hillside. Dilly rested his chin on his arms on the front seat. "Ma'am?" he asked softly. "How far along are you in karate?"

"Brown belt," she murmured. Her mind still seemed to be fixed on the meal she was about to prepare. "I can scramble eggs for you, if you'd like. Yes, maybe that's best after all the excitement. And then there's that lemon meringue pie I baked this afternoon. . . ."

Meanwhile
some distance from the smashed opening . . .

men emerged from a door concealed deep within a ravine. Moving furtively, looking over their shoulders, they gathered under clouds scudding past a waning moon.

Master Operative Gorey was the last to arrive. He stepped from among a clump of bushes. "Report!" The word exploded like a gunshot in the silence.

"Blunt here. Sir!"

"O'Mallet here. Sir!"

"Jep, er, Whir—I mean McHammer here, Unc—I mean Sir!"

The master operative acknowledged them with a brusque nod. "As you know, we are in Phase One of a removal operation. We will proceed to Rendezvous Crocodile."

Blunt spoke. *"Von Pfist has not yet arrived."*

"I doubt that she will." Gorey's voice was grim. *"She did not call Contacts to affirm steps leading to delivery of the note to the bank. I believe she informed someone of our plan."*

"Defected!" O'Mallet's voice was filled with horror, contempt.

"That is the only explanation for the arrival of the boy's bodyguard and guardian."

"But, but," stammered McHammer. *"I don't understand. It was all so simple. How can it have gone wrong?"*

Dr. Keenwit stepped into the moonlight. *"I will tell you what went wrong. That boy, that rich boy, picked up to finance our operation, possesses some strange scientific knowledge which I do not yet fully understand. He destroyed the Great"—* he gave a strangled sob—*"Harmonizer. Have any of you any idea of how long it will take me to"—* the words rose to a wail—*"construct another synchronizer of such complexity?"*

The operatives stood, heads bowed, humiliated by their failure, awed by the enormity of the task facing their leader.

Dr. Keenwit pulled himself together. His next words were harsh. *"But I will. I WILL! The master plan exists in this greatest of all computers."* He touched his forehead. *"My brain. And I will* recover the disks stored in my library. Even if they fall into hostile hands, they will be meaningless. No one can break my code. And so I say, I will recover the disks. I will proceed with my plan." He looked around at them. Moonlight reflected off the whites of the bulging eyes. He rubbed his hands. "Are you with me?"

The master operative was the first to speak. "Aye. With you."

Blunt responded. "Yes. With you."

O'Mallet answered. "In fact. With you."

They turned to McHammer. He had seated himself on a rock and was fingering a leafy stem he had pulled from the ground. "Oh, assuredly, sir. With you. I do hope you have a place for someone like me in your organization, eager to work hard, to learn."

Dr. Keenwit swung around toward the master operative. "Didn't the suggestion that we take that miserable boy come from this, this . . ." He stopped, at a loss for words.

Master Operative Gorey shuffled his feet. He looked down. "Well, yes, it, uh, did."

Dr. Keenwit thrust his face close to Gorey's. "In your excellent work with me, you have rarely bungled. But I ask you now, where did you find this bumbling candidate for operative status, this McHammer."

The master operative's voice was low. "A bright boy. My sister's son. I'm sure he can be trained."

Dr. Keenwit groaned. "Well, train him, then! But keep him out of sensitive operations. And you might start by pointing out to him that he is handling poison ivy."

Turning away, he said, "Proceed to rendezvous point." Then he seemed to remember something. "Your sources? They have no way of tracing you?"

"No way," Master Operative Gorey assured him. "They were paid on the spot, and they have no way of finding us even if they are so inclined. We always made the meeting arrangements."

"Well, at least that part of this general bunglement was handled according to procedure," Dr. Keenwit snapped. "Pickup will take place at three a.m. I hope you have sufficient wits to be there on time."

He paced away among the trees.

Behind him, the operatives synchronized their watches. Then they turned up the collars of their coats, pulled their hats lower over their eyes, and dispersed. They followed their customary cautious procedures.

"*BLACKPOOL AND I* have been talking," said Mr. Orbed.

All eyes turned to him.

Everybody was gathered around the table. Not the table in the window alcove. That was too small. They sat at the big table in the center of the dining room. Mrs. Blackpool bustled in and out, bringing platters of food, passing dishes, pouring milk.

"We've decided to go out and pick up the bull-dozer," he said. "We'll leave here at four o'clock tomorrow morning. With luck, we'll manage to return it to the construction site before the day's work starts up."

Everyone had stopped eating. Exclamations rippled around the table. "Can I go with you?" "I can help you." "Me too." "All of us can help you."

"All of you can sleep in tomorrow morning," Mr. Orbed said calmly.

A groan swept around the table.

"Except for Matthew," Mr. Orbed continued. "Blackpool can load the bulldozer on its trailer and drive it. But we may need direction from Matthew." He turned to Matt. "And you'll have to show us where to deliver it."

Pride showed on Matt's face.

Suddenly Jessica's face lit. "If you take the bulldozer back, I won't have to tell my father what we did." She looked around the table triumphantly. Her eyes met Dr. McEvoy's.

"Do you really want to not tell him?" Dr. McEvoy asked mildly.

"Yes!" Jessica squirmed even as she said it, looking down into her lap, twisting her fingers. Her hair swung forward and hid her face. "But I know I have to." The words were tinged with misery.

"Well now," said Mr. Orbed. "I made a promise to you earlier this evening. I keep promises."

Head tilted, Jessica looked up into the softly shining eyes.

"We'll figure out the least damaging way to tell him about the whole business," said Mr. Orbed.

Jessica's face settled into a smile. "I think I'd like some more roast beef," she said demurely. "And are there any baked beans left?"

"Dr. Mac," asked Bryan, "what happened to that

woman you said told you about Dilly? I mean, where is she now?"

"I sent her to stay with friends of mine at Red Fox Lake," said Dr. McEvoy. "She felt she was in danger from Dr. Keenwit." She glanced over their heads at Mr. Orbed. They exchanged a look of understanding. "That's something else to be done tomorrow. We must talk to her."

"It was because of her that you could get things rolling, even before Bryan called Mr. Blackpool to tell him where we were heading with the bulldozer," said Matt.

"I sure am glad you and Mr. and Mrs. Blackpool met us, sir," Bryan said to Mr. Orbed. "We didn't think about what we were going to do after Matt took apart the side of the hill with the bulldozer."

"We didn't even know how we were going to get it past that fence without setting off an alarm," said Matt, "if there was one."

"Seeing the bulldozer coming through the wall was awesome," said Dilly.

"Awrrr," moaned Contrary. He lifted his empty dish in his mouth.

"Still not filled up, boy?" asked Dilly, taking the dish and adding roast beef to it. He held it above Contrary's nose. "Say 'please'?"

Contrary lay down and covered his eyes with his paws.

"Oh, well," said Dilly, setting the dish on the floor, "you can't blame me for trying. Maybe someday you'll get it right."

DILLY WAS CURLED UP IN BED, watching the endless track of the planets around the sky lamp. He was warm. He was filled up on lemon meringue pie. He was altogether content.

The pillow-lined basket on the floor was empty. Contrary, comfortably full of roast beef, stretched out on the bed at Dilly's feet. He lay without stirring, his eyes open, fixed on Dilly.

There was a tap on the door. Dr. McEvoy, framed by the light in the hall, looked into the room. "I would imagine you're too big for tucking in," she said.

"Well, yeah," Dilly agreed.

"So are Jessica and Matt and Bryan. I just found that out." She chuckled, coming into the room. Crossing it, she seated herself on the window seat and didn't speak for a long moment, looking out into the branches of the tree outside the window. "It's been a day with so many things in it," she said at last. Then, "We couldn't talk in front of the others at supper."

"The kids didn't figure out there's something different about me," said Dilly. "I mean, they didn't catch on about why the lights went out, that I did it."

Dr. McEvoy shook her head. Moonlight struck silver sparks off her hair. "That's apparent from their talk this evening. They only saw that you were in trouble and leaped in to help you. What good friends you have, Dilloway! But tell me, now that we're alone. What's the story about that computer? Even in the poor light I could see that it was big. The set-up had to be highly sophisticated."

Dilly sat up, his arms around his knees. He told her about the Great Harmonizer and the disk library and Dr. Keenwit and his plans.

She listened, increasingly sober. "So there was more to all this than their simply taking you for ransom," she said finally. "It's appalling! You can't handle it. Nor can I. We'll have to leave it to Mr. Orbed. But getting back to the computer—what did you call it? The Great Harmonizer?"

Dilly remembered the music, the changing colored waters of the fountain, the painting. He especially remembered Dr. Keenwit's words telling him what the Great Harmonizer could do. "It sure was a spectacular computer," he said. "I knew I'd hurt it if I sent a power surge into the connections. I sort of didn't want to. Only, Dr. Keenwit was the scariest guy I ever met. I was more scared of what he was going to do with the Great Harmonizer than I was of what might happen to me when I let out that big blast."

"That took courage," said Dr. McEvoy. "Ah, but you're brave, Dilloway. And thoughtful. I couldn't be more proud of you."

She sat there smiling at him and Dilly felt as though he was splashed with sunlight.

"But you still should go through the exercises I outlined," she continued, "building your output slowly. Blacking out shouldn't have to be part of your expectations when you release at peak. But of course you won't do that often. After all, there can't be that many Great Harmonizers in the world!"

She got up from the window seat and came to sit on the edge of the bed. Contrary moved closer to her. "After you came upstairs to bed, Mr. Orbed and I talked about something. We've discussed it before."

Something in Dilly responded to the changed tone of her voice. He hugged his knees more tightly, studying her face in the dim light.

"I wonder how you'd feel if I moved in here and lived with you. A sort of unofficial housemother and teacher."

Dilly didn't for a moment take in the full meaning of this astonishing proposal. "But you have to go back to the university. I mean, what about your work?"

"I can apply for extended leave from my seminars," said Dr. McEvoy. "As for the rest, my work is the sort that can be done anyplace, so long as I have pencils and paper to write on and can access into a computer now and then. Those things aren't a problem. But there's something more.

"Dilloway, it's time for you to know that your father's papers, all his research, have been in Mr. Orbed's care since your father died. He's had them in safe keeping in a bank vault. He understood the value, the unique quality, of your father's thinking, you see. I've read some small part of the research, and I must say it's extraordinary. I have a notion of where he was heading, but a great deal of work still must be done. Now, what we're suggesting is that I continue as your teacher, to bring along your understanding of your magnetism and at the same time tutor you in science. Then, as you grow and become deeply grounded in your field, we will work together on your father's ideas. Someday, you'll handle it alone."

Dilly had been listening in wonder. He didn't reply at once. He reached out and touched the sky lamp. "You want to stay here with me," he said slowly, thinking. With a finger he traced the W of Cassiopeia's Chair. "And teach me." He scarcely dared believe this conversation. "And see my father's work." It was too much to comprehend all at once.

"Ah, Dilloway." Dr. McEvoy's voice was soft. "That's only part of it. I want to do it for a reason that has nothing to do with your father's work. You see, I am, simply, extraordinarily fond of you. I want you to be happy. I want you to—grow. And I want to be part of that growing and happiness."

A comet exploded into brightness and skimmed around the sky lamp.

Dilly felt as though he was riding that comet. A smile crinkled his face. "I'd like that a lot, Dr. Mac," he said simply. "You're the neatest lady I ever met."

"And that's the neatest thing anyone has ever said to me, Dilloway," said Dr. McEvoy, laughing lightly. She reached out and tweaked his big toe. Contrary lifted his head and she gave him an affectionate pat. "Think things over. There's plenty of time for decisions."

She rose and moved toward the door. "As I said, it's been a day with lots of things in it. Get some sleep now."

After she left, Dilly stretched out flat on his back, balancing his pillow on his stomach. He felt as light as one of the feathers in the pillow. Today had been both the worst and the best day of his entire life.

"You know, Con," he said somewhere deep in his mind, "being kidnapped is the most terrible thing that can happen to you."

Agreed, came the unspoken reply. *It was rough on me, too, you know. So please let's not do that anymore.*

"And you know," Dilly went on, "it was scary to zap the Great Harmonizer when I didn't know what would happen to me if I let loose that terrific blast." That brought another thought to mind. "I've kept wondering what use my magnetism was. I mean, what made it better than a circus trick. Today I found out. I can use it to do good things."

Contrary seemed to agree. *That was heavy on my mind. I'm glad we got it worked out.*

Dilly's eyes closed. He breathed deeply. Then his eyes snapped open. "But I guess the best thing that's ever happened to me was Dr. Mac telling me she likes me a lot."

Contrary yawned. *And you telling her how much you like her.*

"And another thing . . ." Dilly's eyelids drooped.

Please no more things, came the answer. *A dog's got to get some sleep, you know.*

"All right, then," Dilly murmured. "Stay awake. See if I care."

His eyes closed. He didn't see that Contrary's eyes had closed, too. They slept, Dilly and Contrary, in the gentle glow of the sky lamp.